The Heart and Other Strangers

Selected Titles by
MORRIE RUVINSKY

Books

Dream Keeper (novel)
Meeting God or Something Like It (short stories)
A Father's Son (novel)

Movies

The Plastic Mile
Improper Channels
The Windsor Protocol
Going to Kansas City
Rainy Days, Rainy Nights
A Woman Hunted

Episodic TV

Myth Quest
Highlander
Misfits of Science

The Heart and Other Strangers

Selected Titles by
MORRIE RUVINSKY

Books

Dream Keeper (novel)
Meeting God or Something Like It (short stories)
A Father's Son (novel)

Movies

The Plastic Mile
Improper Channels
The Windsor Protocol
Going to Kansas City
Rainy Days, Rainy Nights
A Woman Hunted

Episodic TV

Myth Quest
Highlander
Misfits of Science

The Heart and Other Strangers

Morrie Ruvinsky

STORY THREAD PRESS

SANTA MONICA, CALIFORNIA

The Heart and Other Strangers / Morrie Ruvinsky – 1st ed.
Library of Congress Control Number: 2018906008
ISBN-13: 978-0-9903098-2-6

Story Thread Press
Santa Monica, California
www.storythreadpress.com

For my mother and my father,
exemplars of true love (n.o.e.e.),
the first I ever knew.

Contents

Contents

THE BARE NAKED MOURNING
OF MAMA LEBEAU

Everybody gets to die, usually without much practice. It's pretty much one and done.

Mourning, however, is an endless cascade of rehearsals that no one ever gets much better at. A daily business that can take a whole lifetime.

As often happens in periods of great stress, people get to believing a little too hard. They get to thinking that the agonies and madness they've been feeling aren't just a random buzzing in their brain, but a message of true import. And who else could it be from but God.

It happened to Shirley Lebeau. It hadn't come to light in any public way until a motorcycle cop stopped her and seventeen naked members of her family in a nine-car convoy to Texas.

It's the kind of story you might catch while waiting for something else to load on your cell and you think well there's one crazy lady. Maybe you even chuckle to yourself, and you move on.

But Shirley couldn't. She wasn't crazy, she was just in soul-freezing agony, broken by what proved to be unbearable pain.

It happened so quickly. The universe shifted on its axis. When a neighbor, in the company of the police, came to bring her the horrifying news that Harry was dead – unfortunately enmeshed in steel and concrete – something in Shirley went with him.

"No, Katrina," Shirley protested, "it's a mistake. He just left here a few minutes ago."

"Can we go inside?"

"No, Katrina, absolutely not. Do not come in here."

"Shirl—"

"Ever. Do not ever come here again. Ever. Do you understand me! You can't go around scaring the crap out of people!"

Katrina left the cops outside and ushered the newly minted widow back into the house. "I know," Katrina said knowing full well she had no idea what she knew but it was somehow the right thing to say.

"No. No no no," Shirley cried out, losing confidence. "It can't be."

Life without Harry was not just empty, it was inconceivable. They had been inseparable all their lives, if you count the beginning as Junior year in high school when she surrendered her virginity to him and they fell permanently in love. Fairy tale stuff.

"I'm so sorry," Katy assured her, holding her hands.

"Please Katy, no," she pleaded. "Please."

"I know," Katy answered, from the heart, getting the hang of it.

Shirley's guilt was immediate and crushing. "It's my fault," she managed to blurt out. "I didn't even say goodbye."

"I know."

"He must have thought..." she began to say but couldn't. He must have thought I was going to leave him. He died all alone. And it was her fault.

She'd said some awful things that morning when they were fighting. He had to know she wasn't going to leave him even if she was screaming shit at him. He had to know the harsh killer-words were meant only for the ring, only for the combat. He had to know that he meant everything in the world to her, but apparently forgot when he drove into the wall.

Before the accident, Shirley was just Shirley. A little over-worked. A little overwhelmed. Generally happy, reliable. She was a good friend and listener, which had always drawn people to her. They called it her magnetism.

You couldn't have picked her out of a milling mob of moms even with a program. She was just ordinary and normal. In her world it was a great virtue of very high order. She was just one of the guys, the good guys, and she loved it.

It wasn't a Stepford thing, and she wasn't hypnotized by drugs or propaganda, she was simply living a comfortable, decent and generous life. She took care of her family, helped in the church and served in the community all because she wanted to. It was fulfilling and satisfying and she thought it would never change.

The perfect marriage came apart like a wobbling cartwheel. Harry lost his license – caught with his finger in a patient – and the job market for disgraced dentists is very limited. He searched for work but even Uber wouldn't let him drive.

Shirley stood by him. Supported him. Denied with him. Even as they ate up their savings. It was inevitable, feeling broken like he did, that the day would come when he couldn't get it up. Or keep it up. For Harry it was the last sign he needed that he was a done deal. Harry Lebeau was on empty, a worthless asshole who couldn't even get his dick to pay attention.

He thought a lot about dying, the relief it would bring, not only to himself, but to Shirley, and everyone else really. Once the Crown Prince of a devoted family, he now considered himself one lame fuck.

"I'd be better off dead," he told her.

Shirley slapped him. Hard. It was all instinct and reflex. Even before the hand made actual contact she was very, very sorry she had hit him but it was way too late to stop it.

Whack! It left marks.

"Oh my God, Oh my God," she cried out, "I'm sorry. I'm so sorry."

"You asked me what I was thinking!" Harry protested.

"But not that. How could you say something like that to me!"

"I was trying to tell you it feels like I lost the will to live."

Whack!

Wow, she thought, impressed by her reflexes.

And crushed by the look in his eyes. He wasn't angry or hurt or sad or anything else she could recognize. It was a lifeless stare, not even cold, just far away.

She tried to reach for him but he turned away.

He got into his car and ten minutes later he drove into the cement wall by the car wash.

In all the years they'd been together, neither of them had ever left the house without – at the very least, a quick goodbye, or back in twenty, or I love you or fill the tank or pick up some milk. Drive careful. Something.

It had started just because it was nice. It soon became a habit, one they enjoyed and practiced, and then a ritual and finally a deeply embedded superstition. If you don't say *something* – a dozen eggs, carpet tacks from the hardware, see you later – then something terrible was bound to happen.

On that day they had parted in silence. No drive safely, no milk, nothing at the cleaners. Now she was so cornered by guilt that there was barely room for her to grieve or mourn in any way that eased the painful emptiness or mitigated her responsibility.

The agony of blame was too much to bear alone and she turned to her church. She started going regularly but the comfort only lasted while she was sitting there, staring at Jesus.

After a while she began to feel like the crucified Christ staring back at her probably had more on his mind at the moment than her shattered soul and she stopped going.

But she never stopped believing. She read books and listened to sermons and went to lectures by all manner of spiritual explorers and guides, and they all made perfect sense. She began holding meetings at home. And eventually services. Her break with her church was more practical than official.

She felt like Job, beset by overwhelming injustices, but the part where Job suffers without complaint, well that wasn't Shirley. Or, as she was more often now called, *Mama*.

One day she realized that to cleanse her tortured soul there was a model to follow. She would, like Jesus, like Moses, go out into the wilderness and face her demons. Forty days and forty nights. You go out there, just you and God. You pour out all your pain and you come back whole. Or blessed.

The desert called and she answered.

She suffered the blistering days and the surprisingly cold nights. She gave herself to the desert, the contemplation and the earnest impulse to let herself off the hook.

She gave it her best shot but it really wasn't working so she only stayed three days. She came home more lonely than before. She was in desperate need of forgiveness, redemption, but most especially, release from the consuming emptiness inside her.

It was, she thought at the time, the nadir of her life. It also was probably the half-starving from the half-fasting in the desert, but that first night home she got the vision.

No mistaking it. No escaping it. Not if she was going to make things right with Harry.

But this is more than just a story about Shirley and some cop who also happens to get messages. Maybe there's no moral to it but it sure is curious to see how God can get into someone's brain and get Himself stuck there.

Corporal John Luke Mathews, a motorcycle cop, was known to his very few friends as Hey.

He was worn out, a man whose life had taken a very bad turn. He lost everyone he loved in an instant, and hasn't known a moment of peace in a long time.

A scary guy, he walked softly and carried a very short fuse. Way too many years on a bike vibrating his kidneys and his balls eight hours a day had left him on the verge of a newsworthy local explosion.

The world would know none of this if Mathews hadn't stopped Lew Bernstein for speeding. Eighty-two miles an hour! Hell, Mathews chuckled to himself, we got wheelchairs around here that go faster than that. But they don't have New York plates.

"Son," Mathews says to him, "you must think you're awful important, driving like that."

Bernstein apologizes. Three or four times. It's as if he knows he's standing beside unstable ammunition.

"Eighty-two in a forty-five mile zone, Son, that's big trouble." He says it with a lilting southern sociability. Like he's your good buddy. Relaxes people, throws them off guard.

"Forty-five?"

"Forty-five." Mathews had no idea how fast Bernstein was driving, he had no speed gun, no mileage markers, no tail. But the line had held up now for years because everyone who isn't from the south is scared of Southern cops and dare not dispute the charge.

"I didn't see a sign," Bernstein, like so many before him protested.

"Folks here don't need a sign."

"Then how—"

"Well Son, I guess they just have the sense to know when they're going too fast, especially in a place where they don't belong." Very little gave Mathews pleasure anymore. Fucking over Yankees was one of the most reliable.

The more he made them squirm, the more he felt. That was the goal, to feel something. It was a Yankee did this to him, and puny revenge was his only option.

"Won't happen again," Bernstein promised hopefully.

"The thing is, you're a stranger around here and it would be hard to expect you to know the local laws. I hear you people have your own laws."

"You people?"

"Let me understand this, Son, you're in a hurry to get somewhere, is that right?"

"No, sir." The relief in Bernstein's heart was vile and racist. He thought: he's not going to shoot me because I'm not black. But I'm just as scared as if I were.

"I'm asking if you got some sign from Jesus telling you to drive through here like that...in that fancy car."

"Cars were passing me like I was standing still."

"Must feel terrible I picked you out. God works in mysterious ways," he growled, and then kicked Bernstein's tire. Hard. "Mysterious fucking ways," he emphasized.

"Can I just pay my fine and put this behind me. No receipt, no memory." He held his breath, anticipating disaster. It is always a bad idea to try to bribe an honest cop.

"Ticket like this run you close to three hundred dollars plus whatever your insurance company's going to tack on because of it. Could be an even bigger bite than the ticket," Mathews warned, resigned that playtime was over and they were down to business.

"So you're thinking what, two hundred?" Bernstein ventured.

"No, I was thinking you really don't want to spend the night in my jail."

"I've got two-hundred-and-eighty-three dollars," Bernstein tells him, and shows him his wallet.

Mathews considered for a moment if he should just kill him. He'd been thinking for a long time now that he should shoot someone. Anyone. Just to get the horrors in his brain to go away. Blow something up instead of himself.

"You got family?" he asked Bernstein in an attempt to dissuade himself.

Bernstein never got a chance to answer A long convoy of nose-to-tail vehicles pulled up on the grass.

People were singing and it seemed only a little strange that no one exited their vehicles for the longest time. Mathews was curious of course, but not yet alarmed, until Mama Lebeau stepped out of her camper.

Shirley was stark naked and the trooper immediately drew his gun.

"Now, now," she laughed, walking straight toward him, "you put that nasty thing away."

He obeyed without hesitation and turned his eyes away.

"You can look," she told him. Her voice was plain. Straight forward. "Don't be afraid. You can look."

She was stunning. A little heavier than she needed to be perhaps, and sort of tired and road-weary, but charismatically radiant. The trooper was so smitten he couldn't look.

"I could feel you, even as we were coming up the road," she told him.

"Feel me?"

"Your pain."

"My back? You mean my back. No, that's pretty much over. Do I know you?"

"One way to tell is by looking at me."

He tried.

"Lose someone?" she asked with such genuine concern that even Bernstein was moved.

Trooper John's inability to answer, to speak, was enough.

"Me too," she said.

"We're all like this," she told him, moving just a little closer. She motioned lightly with her hand and others emerged from their vehicles. All as naked as advertised.

The trooper hadn't seen a naked woman since the accident and this was all too much.

"I had a vision," she told the trooper.

"I'm going to have to arrest you all if you don't go and put some clothes on right this minute. Now go on and make yourselves decent."

Nobody laughed but they did ignore him. Some lay in the grass just enjoying being alive. A couple were halfway up the hill yelling at each other while a young man stood by trying to hide his stubbornly erect shame.

"I'm serious. Tell them to get dressed."

"I had a vision."

"Yes, Ma'am."

"And when I woke up I was lying on the floor, on my back, and I cried with joy."

"You still have to get dressed."

"You still have to look at me."

So he did and all he saw was her eyes.

"There," she said.

He blushed.

"I was on a mountain. In Texas, a place I never been to, but it felt familiar, like I should be there," she explained.

"Is someone waiting for you?"

"Yes!" How did he know? She was deeply moved. It was another sign that her vision was exactly what she hoped it was: Harry was waiting for her.

"Ma'am, I'm still going to—"

"Reverend."

"Ma'am?"

"Reverend. Reverend Lebeau. They all call me Mama."

"Mama?"

"Not you. Not yet."

"Okay."

"It was like Moses and the Burning Bush, I hear this voice and I know right away who it is. Big, big voice."

"Was there a burning bush?" the trooper asked.

She was not offended but she stared at him for a while. "No," she said, "a waterfall."

"Oh."

"Shed the skins that hide the soul, and you shall be free."

"Shed the skins?"

"Shed the skins. Don't you see? The clothes that hide us from each other and trap the soul in shame."

"You sure it wasn't sins?"

"What?"

"Sins. Shed your sins."

She thought about it. "No, I'm pretty sure it was skins." It better be, it's what propelled this entire quest. Life was a whole lot easier when she was just Shirley. She longed to be just Shirley again, but without Harry she didn't know who that was.

"Ma'am. Reverend Ma'am, I'd sell my soul for a vision."

"Keep your soul," she said and took his hand and led him back to her camper. You'd have thought to see some expression of, say surprise, because these were very Christian folk, but nobody seemed to notice or mind. The few that did, smiled.

After about ten minutes, the camper door opened and the trooper's clothes came hurtling out. They were in there for an hour and it is not difficult to imagine what might have transpired in that camper, inspired in part by the occasional moaning. But that is not what went on at all. These were people who trusted in the healing powers of purity.

They sat opposite each other, naked and a little afraid. Both of them broken by tragedy, each of them consumed by it. She held his hands and asked only this of him: "Look into my eyes."

They held hands and felt each other's pain. Understood each other's despair. Without a word they confessed their agonies.

He cried out in helpless surrender and he wept. She could not. After an hour, they were both spent, and well satisfied. He believed she was his salvation. She believed he was sent to guide her to the promised land.

Mathews emerged from the camper with his mind clear and the ache in his soul erased. He had become pristine. Stark naked but for his boots, he marched straight over to Bernstein who looked like he thought he was about to be re-circumcised.

"I am saved," Mathews announced to Bernstein, "and I know now that Jesus sent you to show me the way—"

"No he didn't."

"And I tremble in shame for how I treated you." He knelt naked before Bernstein and bowed low.

"Don't do that," Bernstein pleaded.

"I am forever grateful."

"Get up."

"I have never known a Messenger before."

"It was all part of the plan," Bernstein assured him.

One might anticipate that a caravan of uncovered Christians led by a naked Trooper from a neighboring state would get a little more respect in Texas than most other places. Texas, after all.

The Reverend Mama Lebeau sensed early on that crossing the Line into the Lone Star state was not the paradise they'd been craving. In fact, some folks were downright hostile.

"Why is he slowing down!" she muttered as Mathews slowed to a crawl.

"Praise the Lord!" he shouted at six miles an hour, forcing the rest of the caravan to become a parade.

"Oh, Jesus," she muttered. She didn't know what to do. Harry would have known. He'd have put a stop to it.

Mathews was quite a sight, but with much too much detail for this town: A State Trooper, wearing nothing but his boots, riding no-hands because his arms were spread wide in crucifixional fashion.

It must have felt like a powerful a sign to Mathews when the local cops pulled him over right in front of City Hall and not on some dark road or rotting alley or out on the plains where you could go thirty miles without seeing another human being or similar species.

Filled with the glory of God and the gospel witness of the Right Reverend Mama Lebeau, Mathews leapt from his bike and ran halfway up the broad steps of government where he turned to face his pursuers.

He called out in joy, "Come to Jesus, don't make Jesus come to you!"

Stopped everyone in their tracks.

It was not so much the blasphemy as the erection.

There were a growing number of cops, but not one of them wanted to be the first to tackle the guy with the woody. As an erection, it wasn't all that spectacular. Pretty good, but not great. Obviously functional however and this was a situation no one wanted to be the first to touch.

It was not the erection per se that was the problem, so much as the context. It is not considered polite to display one in Texas where the men are all cowed enough by having seen a bull or two at stud.

Mathews was shivering but insistently naked. By the will of God his arms spread in welcome never tired. The erection embarrassed him a little, but if this is what God wants, this is what God wants.

None of the local cops – except for the two women – seemed able to look directly at him, and they only glanced. At first. The shorter one was having a harder and harder time looking away. It had been too long since she'd been this close to a live cock and thought, just for a fleeting moment, which is of course all it takes, that maybe this guy really was somehow sent by God. He had an Alabama accent after all.

"Could someone," the taller women barked, "get this asshole a blanket before I shoot his dick off."

But not even that could dent his proud display of manly determination. This was God speaking. Here among the heathens, he finally figured it out. He was John the Baptist, called to spread the word, and suffer whatever the Lord required of him.

"Come to me," he said. Naked and unafraid.

The cops, all seven or eight of them by now, were stumped and kept their distance. "I'll get the blanket," the short infatuated cop announced. She was excited about being assigned a job that obligated her to get a little closer.

Transformed by the angel Lebeau and her holy teachings about the body being a sacred temple, Trooper Mathews offered what he could. "Come suck my holy dick," he cried out.

In Texas.

"What did you say!"

"It'll change your life," Mathews pressed on.

The cops were stymied. They wanted to kill him but knew instinctively that the *I-thought-he-was-going-to-piss-on-me* defense might not hold up. Really confusing to know what to do to a naked perp with a religious hard-on.

Mama Lebeau had a sense of how quickly innocence can turn to horror. She grabbed her bible and ran across the lawn screaming. "Don't shoot! Don't shoot!"

As it turns out, one naked person is a dilemma. Two screaming naked people shifts the balance drastically. Suddenly the cops felt under attack. Suddenly it was self-defense.

Of course Mama Lebeau was not alone. She was joined by fifteen or so naked devotees rushing to her side. It's not hard to imagine that this might have played out differently in Malibu, but in Texas it was a worst nightmare – after the *Walking Dead* – and they responded the only way they knew how. They opened fire.

It was ferocious. All shooting at the same time, it sounded more like a cannon than a fusillade. The explosive noise knocked birds from the sky.

They emptied their guns and rifles. Eighty-seven shells and casings were later recovered. No one reloaded. No one dared to move.

It resembled nothing so much as a practiced tableau, until the Mayor came running down the steps yelling, "What the hell! What the hell!"

"God will call you to account for this," Mama Lebeau said glaring at him.

"Yes, Ma'am," he said, keeping his eyes well-mannered. He was immediately aware that he was in way over his head. He could see over her shoulder, two of his officers removing their clothes in solidarity.

Of all the guns unloaded in fear, anger and reflex, not a single one of Mama's flock was hit.

Not a single one. No one hurt at all except for little Ralphito who tripped and skinned his knee.

"It's unbelievable," the Mayor muttered, still stunned by the failure of half a year's worth of ammunition. "They all shot into the air!"

"Maybe," Mama Lebeau offered an out, "maybe here in Texas folks don't cotton to shooting Christians."

"I don't see why not, Ma'am, no offense intended."

"I understand. This is a decent town with decent folk and I can see where folks might see us as invading hippies or—"

"Yes, Ma'am."

"But we're just Christians," she explained, "every one of us, on our way to a baptism we have long prepared for."

"Yes, Ma'am, but you are all—"

"Doing God's will. There is no abomination going on here. No gutter business. We shed our clothes to honor our devotion to His will. <u>His</u> will. Now, there are a lot of things you're allowed to do in Texas that you aren't allowed to do in some other places. And there are some things in Texas you just can't do. First among them is you can't deny God's will."

So the Mayor listened to Mama Lebeau very carefully and when she began to describe the promised land she was looking for, she hit gold.

"Grimer's Climb," he announced.

She had never heard the name before but it resonated so perfectly she felt the blood rush to her brain, all cells firing. "You know this place!"

"Everyone around here does. Giant pine tree you said?"

"Biggest Norfolk Pine I ever saw."

"And the only one for forty miles," he told her, cementing his claim.

"Yes! Yes!" her heart soared. Yes.

"It's no tree," he revealed, "it's a cellphone tower!"

"Yes," she cried out. "I knew it."

It was like every fiber in her body tingled with the realization that they were here. Actually, factually, here. No dreaming, no more doubts. Her faith had seen her through and offered up this extraordinary reward. Hallelujah! Hallelujah! Hallelujah.

"Grimer's Climb," the Mayor shrugged, "can't be more than an hour away but it's hardly worth the drive."

"Thank you," Mama said. She went in for a hug but he backed away.

"I can tell you right now, much as I want you out of my town, that's forlorn country out that way. Whatever you're looking for, you're not gonna find it there."

Mama had no time to debate with him so she said yes to everything. He won't have anyone arrested, he'll give her directions to Grimer's Climb – more of a hill than a mountain really – and in return Mama Lebeau and all her people would put their clothes on and keep them on as long as they're in Texas.

Grimer's Climb turned out to be three hours away and it was indeed forlorn. There was no one else at the campgrounds, not a ticket taker or a groundskeeper or water or electricity, in spite of the cell tower.

It was already dark by the time they made camp and settled in. Had dinner. Just chilling because Ma-

ma had not told them that this was in fact their desti-
nation, as in the old-fashioned sense of destiny.

She had to be sure first.

After everyone had gone to sleep she snuck out
and made the climb. There was a pretty big moon up
so it was easy to find her way. Couldn't have taken
more than half an hour or so to get to the top but it
felt like a very, very long time in light of what she
expected to find.

It really was a hill and not a mountain, but everything around it was so flat it was promoted by default.
She stepped lightly when she at last reached the
meadow, with tentative steps, like she imagined Moses approaching the fire, or Gandhi the British.

Forlorn or not, the view was appropriately awesome. It was a very good sign, and she didn't know
what to do. Just stand there and wait? Pray? What?
She had come this far and there was no reason to be
anything but direct.

"Harry," she whispered.

In the city, one hardly notices, but out here in
places like this, of which there are not that many left,
even a half-moon sheds enough light to see the world.
Nothing was going to sneak up on her.

"Harry." Her voice barely audible above the whispering grasses. "Harry."

Nothing. Nothing. She began to panic. A few deep breaths stayed the adrenalin, and as she began to settle the problem became obvious. It was the clothes. Shed the skins, she reminded herself. The deal with God had been clear from the beginning. Shed your skins. Screw the Mayor.

The joy she felt as she discarded her clothes was unlike anything she had ever experienced before. Even at that first revelation. She could feel herself absorb the Universe.

She could feel Harry, barely a breath away.

She stood bathed in lunar splendor, dedicated and devoted, stripped to her sinless soul, arms spread in invitation, "I'm here, my love," she called out.

And no one responded. There was no answer. No shift in the breeze. No new dazzle in the stars. No surge in her heart. It all collapsed in an instant. Her noble mission reduced to a very long wail of agony.

"You lying son of a bitch!" she hollered.

It wasn't Harry she was screaming at. It was God, and there was nowhere to hide from her fury in the cloudless sky.

"I trusted you!" She was devastated.

The silence was now emptier than it had ever been.

"Fuck you," she roared. "And your son if he's with you!"

She picked up a stone to hurl at God's face, but couldn't find it. A wail of immense betrayal cloaked the night.

"I did everything you asked me to, night after night, dream after dream, prayer after prayer," she howled in frustration still looking for where to throw her stone. She wanted to get Him right in the eye. "I bared my naked body and bore the shame."

She paced angrily and finally just dropped the stone. "I believed and I dragged people I love halfway across the country because You put this ugly mountain in my head."

She went back and got the stone. "What is wrong with You!"

Back in her camper, Mama Lebeau continued to massage her midnight revelations. After all the extraordinary sacrifices and humiliation, it was over. All for naught. She had no idea what she was going to tell everyone, and she especially had no idea what to do with a god-soaked motorcycle cop. And then there was explaining it back home, and living in ridicule for the rest of their lives.

Dawn was coming soon enough and maybe it would bring answers. In the meantime she was lost, and it filled her heart with a sadness she hadn't dared feel before.

She crawled into bed and wept. And in her tears, she found Shirley.

Just before she fell asleep, she closed her eyes and whispered, "Don't forget the milk."

— ◊ —

A PLACEBO FAIRY TALE

A lot of people are going to think this isn't a true story. Some may even think it's satire, that things like this don't happen anymore. That fairy tales are just make believe – an attitude that stems apparently from the current dearth of mythical horses.

Just to review, it goes like this: A beautiful princess, usually in dire straits, is rescued by a knight in shining armor (usually royal) and is carted off to his castle to bear his heirs and organize the kitchen staff.

In a placebo fairy tale, there are no horses.

So here you go.

1. The Beautiful Princess

Once upon a time, less than four months ago, a charming young woman named Lydia ran a lovely little placebo shop in what used to be her den. The shelves were neatly stocked with all the pills and syrups she might ever need to prescribe, including the infamous Red-striped Hollow. The Hollow – now under threat of discontinuation – was considered the single most dangerous placebo in her entire arsenal, and it was at the center of the very oppressive difficulty in which she currently found herself.

Were she a real princess, she would be beloved. She was kind, generous and treated most of her patients for free. She carried herself with grace and maintained a posture of unfazed pride in public. At home alone, these last few months, she cried a lot and felt ill a lot and her digestion, which was never much to speak of in the first place, was not improving.

Borne with dignity, difficulty was the very core of her life – you can check Fairy Princesses on Wikipedia to verify how difficult it is for them before the guy and the horse show up. Cinderella, Rapunzel, the one with the pea, Tsarena who never ever smiled, and so on.

People marveled at Lydia's stoic demeanor, like an on-duty Royal, and loved her because no matter how hard it might be for her personally, she remained a warm and gracious healer. A true believer herself, her cure rate for some conditions was often better than conventional medical treatment. Bedwetting for example.

In the past year she had cured four unique bed-wetters. Two adults treated with combination therapy – two small sublingual placebos twice a day, in addition to one morning and one evening glucose tablet, which while not actually a prescription drug was not technically a placebo. (She was developing a sugarless sugar pill but so far anecdotal trials have been murky.)

The prepubescent teenager was treated with jujubes. Halloween packs. Licorice and orange only. He scoffed, until he was informed that they had been stolen from the private stash of a Klingon Prince who has now not wet the bed in over two hundred years.

"That's ridiculous," the kid told her.

She ignored it. "The black one in the morning, you chew it very slowly, and the orange one anytime after dinner."

"It's candy."

"Two hundred years, a dry mattress."

"And there's no such thing as Klingons."

"What about the Jonas Brothers," she challenged. "They real enough for you?"

"Which one."

"All of them."

"And you cured them?!"

"We don't say cured. We say dry."

"The Jonas Brothers. Really?"

"It started with the breakup."

"And now?"

"All dry. The middle one has lapses but that's because he forgets his candy sometimes."

Chronic back pain was a big seller. And a lot of digestive issues, and of course straight-forward unvarnished psychological presentations. Her cure rate for bad marriages was astonishing, mostly because she figured those that failed were supposed to and the baby aspirin just helped things along.

Lydia did this all from her house because that's all she had. It was everything she had.

She was born in this house. Raised a family, attended her parents dying in this house, lost her husband in this house.

And now she was going to lose the house too.

2.   *The Bitch and the Seven Dorks*

They were in open court and Lydia's ex, Sandra, was on the witness stand. She was, even Lydia would agree, stunning. Three or four questions in, Sandra exploded. "She's a lying, conniving, bloodsucking bitch."

"I am none of those things, Sandra," Lydia shot back.

"You fleeced me!"

The Judge hammered. "Ladies! Decorum." She was a handsome woman, the judge, and she radiated a gentle confidence and authority.

In the old days the princesses had no former lovers, which gets you to wondering, just why then were they locked up and cast away in towers.

"The Hollow's not worth squat," Sandra announced. "It's just make-believe."

"Please," the judge ordered. "This is not a therapy session, get your ovaries in check."

They were in court because of the seven dorks, small businessmen who along with Lydia owned a very valuable block in the heart of burgeoning Santa Monica. Lydia's house occupied the best corner, but she refused to sell. "This is my home."

The men (Sleepy, Dopey, and so on) had tried persuasion, coercion, lawsuits and mediations, but they couldn't budge Lydia. "Unless you're building a bridge or a freeway through my living room, I'm not moving."

The men had just about given up hope when the Sandra incident unfolded, like a gift from the gods, which the men assumed they deserved because each and every one of them tithed regularly.

Sandra materialized as the incredibly fortuitous witness who changed everything. She and Lydia had had a huge fight and had broken up. Sandra took to the street. That very corner.

She stood in the middle of the intersection. She was crying and her heart was broken, but her god-given beauty and the misfortune of always looking impeccable made it difficult to garner sympathy while gumming up traffic.

Unmoved by all the blaring horns, her focus was entirely on Lydia's second floor bedroom window. In her agony Sandra ripped her shirt open, and exposed her personally designated: *very, very lovely tits.*

It put an immediate stop to the honking. Some in appreciation, others just startled. A couple of pedestrians applauded.

Sandra, who was mostly unaware of her fans, and certainly wasn't listening to them, yelled up at Lydia who was paying no attention, "You'll never see these again!"

Most people were interested in the tits but a couple of dorks – Sneezy and Doc – realized they had just hit the jackpot. Not only was Lydia a woman alone and therefore by definition weak and vulnerable, but she's a fucking lesbian too! Hallelujah. They had an angry ex-lover ripe for the plucking, and they were ready to go back to court.

When Sandra told them about the Red-Striped Hollow and how it had almost killed her, they figured they had the princess by the balls. If they could get her business shut down, maybe even get her a little locked up, she'd have to sell. They were confident enough to re-kindle conversations with former prospective developers.

What made the hand-painted Hollow so dangerous was not just the size, it was the weight. It was empty. As in hollow. Absolutely nothing but air, neatly packaged in a clear gelatin capsule with a hand-painted red stripe.

Of course, the power of the myth (data-based now that people have actually died) was that it could kill you. The Hollow was too big, way too light, and so very very difficult to swallow.

Lydia always warned clients that few people were evolved enough to handle the Hollow and that seemed to incite Sandra. There were horror stories and Lydia shared them freely. Tales of near-fatal choking and of the even more significant actual choking. The rumors were rampant.

By the time Lydia had finished laying out the risks and horrors of the Hollow, Sandra could barely contain herself. "The reward is what?" she demanded as if she weren't already committed.

"Self-esteem," Lydia explained. Over the years she had tried other answers – *it'll cure what ails you; it's good for the organs; prevents Alzheimer's* – but self-esteem was by the far the most preferred. Because with enough self-esteem you can overcome disease, battle failure, conquer fear and maybe even become President of the United States of America.

Seriously.

"Self-esteem! For two thousand dollars—"

"Two thousand five hundred," Lydia quickly corrected.

"Shouldn't I get something tangible for that?"

"Maybe you'll become President."

"What?"

"Nothing." It was their first meeting, their first conversation and it was obviously not going well. After half the morning, they finally agreed to three thousand, eight hundred and fifty-five dollars.

Just to define the ethical boundaries here, the deal was signed, sealed and delivered before they became lovers. By a very pleasant couple of hours.

"The striped Hollow," Lydia had answered for the umpteenth time.

"And all I get is self-esteem? Does it seem to you that I am lacking in self-esteem." She was truly injured. Completely exposed. Very naked.

"That is a lot," Lydia assured her.

Thank God, Sandra reminded herself, I have great tits. "Self-esteem indeed," she huffed, "do these look like a lack of self-esteem," she blurted out pointing at her own, lovely, she must admit, erect nipples.

"No, of course not," Lydia re-assured her, still early in the negotiation. "But twenty-eight hundred dollars is a lot of money."

"Twenty-eight hundred? I thought—"

"And the supplemental charges, is close to six hundred more." Lydia didn't like her and was going to push it as far as she could. Women like her, Lydia rationalized, living lives full of blessings and bounty should be squeezed dry for believing in shit like this.

"Yes," Sandra agreed, reveling in the implied insult for a moment. "It's a lot of money."

"Perhaps," Lydia thought out loud, preparing to close the deal, "you might prefer the creme. It's not quite the same of course, but you get a whole month for under a hundred dollars."

"Money," Sandra scoffed, bleeding pride. "It's not about the money."

"Of course not," Lydia dismissed. "I was just saying that a lot of the girls from Macy's use—"

"Shop girls?"

"Some of them are so lovely," Lydia announced with not a hint of the joyous irony she was feeling, "it's hard to imagine they work for a living."

Lydia treated many of her clients for free, though she hated the term treated. Conversation. It was conversation she offered. But this woman, with the hard nipples and no idea whatsoever why she bought them, this woman deserved to be squeezed. For her arrogance. For her choice of veneer. For her intentional ignorance. For denying her own days as a shop girl. But mostly for thinking Lydia was squeezing her.

Lydia hated being so transparent. She considered transparency highly over-rated. For her it was a consuming burden. She saw too much. She said too much. She felt too much and it was getting to her. She was more tired than usual. Less empathetic than expected.

3.   *The Night Errant*

Lydia's lawyer was a man. Not by choice so much as by tactic. Better to get fucked on a bale of hay than a bed of nails, he told her.

"I have no idea what you just said," she said.

"What I'm saying is, this is a simple case of commercial fraud. She got what she paid for, which was exactly as described, an empty placebo capsule."

"She almost died."

"And you can tell she didn't die because she's testifying against you."

"This is all because we broke up."

"This is not something we want to emphasize."

"Why, are we ashamed of it?"

"That's not the point."

"What is the point?"

"Lesbians don't do well in court."

"I'm not a lesbian," Lydia protested, amused. "And neither is she."

"You were lovers!"

"And that makes us lesbians?"

"The court might think so."

"So because I made love with her, I'm a lesbian."

"I think so."

"Fine. I'm a lesbian and I appreciate getting to find this out."

"You're not taking this seriously."

"I'd love to meet your wife, wink, wink."

"Now you're just fucking with me."

"Oh, was it good for you? It was great for me." She was furious. "My future hangs in the balance here and you can't get your mind out of my crotch."

"These people are trying to destroy your life and I'm all that stands in the way."

"Oh shit."

"Absolutely." It meant that he wouldn't put her on the stand. A combative, angry anybody rarely makes for good legal argument.

Instead, he brought satisfied customers to the stand. People who loved Lydia. People she helped.

People whose lives she made better by sheer force of her caring. People with heartfelt gratitude.

"You went to see her because...?" Lydia's attorney prompted one such customer.

"My uncle."

"Your uncle? Because he was, as I understand it, in great agony?"

"Because he couldn't..." he trailed off.

"He couldn't...?" he coaxed.

"Can I say that in Court? In front of a lady Judge?"

"You would simply be describing a medical condition. Go ahead."

"The man couldn't...shit."

"Excuse me?"

"He was stuffed up like a holiday pig."

"So you went to Lydia's shop for medical supplies."

"No, sir, just the placebos."

"Pills with nothing in them?"

"They had worked for him before."

It went well until it came to the cross. "Sir, I hope your uncle is feeling...more comfortable these days."

"Yes he is."

"And while he was taking these placebos, did he seek any other care?"

"Doctors, of course. He went to the doctor, he's not a fool. He takes the placebos just in case."

"And the doctors give him medicine?"

"Yes, Sir."

"Thank you."

And so it goes and so it went. Every satisfied customer left the stand squealing like a whipped warthog. Not only had they damaged Lydia, pretty much beyond repair, but they'd had their own worlds bashed and collapsed. Some wept as they left knowing they had somehow destroyed a connection to their last line of medical defense, their last option.

It was probably against the rules, but when Lydia recognized that the Judge was developing a headache from the stress, she slipped her a chocolate M&M.

It was in a little plastic pill baggie, with Lydia's name printed on it. In her shop they sold for a dollar a piece. Outside, she gives them away.

The Judge was surprised and even a little offended. She didn't know quite what to do. You can't go around taking gifts from contestants in a trial. It's just not right.

On the other hand, she had a killer headache and it was getting worse and Lydia did seem nice and it was trivial, a goddam M&M and no one saw anyway and so she popped it.

It was in fact her favorite flavor and she took a moment to savor.

Within a few minutes, she felt considerably better.

A few minutes more and the headache was gone, along with any chance the Seven Slicksters had left of winning anything.

4.   *The Horseless Marriage*

Fairy tales can come true. It didn't matter what the lawyers had to say after the M&M, and when all the chattering was done, and all the rules had been followed, the Judge decreed entirely for Lydia.

That alone should qualify as the happy ending for the embattled princess, but there was more.

The greedy bad guys were sent packing. Broken in spirit and pocket, the Seven Settled Suitors (Grumpy, Grabby, Bloodless and the rest) sold their shops, and high-tailed it out of the story.

Then came the dashing Prince on a proud stallion – figure of speech only – to save Lydia from loneliness and despair. Complete with flowing locks. It was the Judge in her brand new big Tesla convertible.

They fell in love over brownies and hot chocolate and at last Lydia was, genuinely happy.

Together they bought up the seven sleepy little shops and sold the block to developers for a staggering sum. Determined that the money be used for good, Lydia opened up free placebo clinics all over the city.

Lydia and the Judge turned out to be a good thing. A real thing. The Judge left the bench and together, they launched a new adventure, bigger and bolder than the last. In storefronts and shopping malls across the country: *Placebo Surgery While-U-Wait.*

It was a no-brainer.

And they lived happily ever after.

So there.

— ◊ —

THE PURPLE ROSE CAFE

Truth is no one really knows what happened to Rose.

Most everyone who ventures into this dinky little café in this otherwise unremarkable little town comes to heal their own shattered hearts. They come because they pretty much buy into the love-addled rumors of Rose and the ghost train.

It all happened way back when, but they still come in search of the promise. Legend has it that the spirit of Rose still lingers and if she warms to you, she'll mend your messed-up life.

So they come in despair. They come broken. They come in feverish anticipation that they might touch a bit of Rose's magic, or catch a glimpse of that blinding spark of perfect love.

It was Parker himself who changed the name from Parker's Place to The Purple Rose Cafe. He did it months after she disappeared, in her honor, not to spike the tourist trade. But it did both. Unintentional consequences.

He posted a picture of a purple rose encased in Lucite that sat on a shelf over in the corner where Rose liked to sit. Didn't say anything about it online, just: "For Rose."

It was meant for friends. Instead it went viral.

He got several hundred hits in the first hour. What Rose? Who's Rose? Go fuck yourself you sick bastard. I don't get it. But mostly he got genuine interest. Personal curiosity.

So he framed and hung a handkerchief embroidered by Rose on a hard-ass day: "If it weren't for the suffering, there'd be no damn need for Heaven."

After all these years it was showing its age, but people brought their own tributes now and tacked them to the walls so they could get a shot of themselves to post, along with their testimonials.

Locals ordered off menu, but tourists usually wanted the Rose Platter, reputed to be a replication of her last meal. It always came with a rose. And if you were there a little before noon, it also came with a song. Same song every day.

> *Delta Dawn,*
> *What's that flower you have on…*

Women tend to weep in solidarity with the desperation of the lyrics, while the men often wondered just what she was trying to say, really.

The Café radiates inspiration. It heals the heart, kindles fires, and assuages guilt. Whatever you need. And there was always the bullshit to leaven the pain. Like the food, Parker just served up whatever he was cooking, stuck a flower in it and called it, always in a whisper, her last meal.

He talked about a lot of things and told a lot of stories. Because he was so generous and easy-going, no one knew how isolated he felt every night going home. Deep down he was a little pissed that Rose seemed to help everyone but him. Never found him anyone. Never healed his broken heart.

The town generally wakes before Parker does. He leaves the place unlocked so early rising regulars can fix their own coffee and toast before he gets there and starts cooking.

"The last time I ever saw her was on that Wednesday," he told a traumatized young woman from Halifax. "She was in a lot of pain. Not just her knees. I'm talking inside. Lot of pain."

Halifax almost teared in empathy but managed not to.

Parker offered her a tissue and poured her some coffee. "I miss her. Sure, she was a little crazy, love, you know, but to me she was fresh air itself. I was just a kid back then. Every time I saw her she had something new to show me, or a way of looking at things that I never thought of before. Broken hearts, she used to say, spill infinite light."

There was no stopping it this time, Halifax wailed. He put a hand on her shoulder and when she was able, she asked, "Were you and she...?"

No, they were not, never had been, not the way she meant.

"Oh. Sorry, I didn't—"

He comforted her with a Rose Platter Special breakfast and she stopped crying and said something about the love of her life being a lying turd and how much she missed him.

"I hear that a lot," he assured her. He never quite understood. People speak of recent exes in the bitterest of terms, and still want to go back. They don't seem to realize they have to give up the good stuff along with the crap they're dumping. It is exactly a case of the baby and the bathwater.

"Oh." She was not alone. That was good to know. Also, it pissed her off a little because she presumed that she was suffering a unique agony. Sharing is one thing, impinging another. All she wanted from Rose was a sign. "Should I go back to him?" she asked Parker.

"Well," he stalled too long.

"No," she clarified, "I mean you knew Rose. What would she say? She'd hate me, wouldn't she?"

"Rose didn't much—"

"Can't blame her."

"Rose believed in love." It was a stock response. Got him out of a lot of tight corners. Rose believed in love.

"The thing is, if I did go back to him it would... well it would kill my husband for one thing."

"Oh," Parker managed. Rose was very big on honor and loyalty and true love and so on, and the truth, were he to tell it, is that Rose would send her packing. Probably wouldn't even let her finish breakfast.

"Three weeks. I've known this man for three weeks and I'm here throwing my life away! Please. Help me."

"You're asking if it's real?"

"Can it happen in an instant?"

"True love?"

"Yes." She was weeping now, she couldn't stop it. "Yes."

"Is that what happened?"

"No. Not really. I mean I like him I suppose. "

"Well," he said, "I guess if you have to ask, maybe it's not what you're looking for."

"Did you just make that up?"

Caught. Trapped. "Sorta," he admitted.

"Thank you," she said, inexplicably moved. Touched that he had gone to the trouble. Her fucking husband never listened.

The last time Rose ever ate breakfast at the diner was never. She always ate breakfast at home. Same thing every day. Corn flakes soaked in apple juice, with just a little hint of vodka and then no drinking until the sun goes down or looks like it's about to or probably will sooner or later.

But she was always there for the early lunch. Before the train. Even that last mythical day. In her regular seat at the counter, a little daisy in her hair. (And for the record, it was often a daisy, sometimes just an autumnal leaf or a single fallen petal, but never a rose.)

"So I started thinking about it," Rose told Parker one day, "and realized there's hardly a problem in the world that can't be fixed by a good story or a song."

"Any particular song?"

"You kidding me, Parker? Me? I could listen to Delta Dawn every day."

She meant it as a tease, a little joke on herself. She knew people thought she was a little addled, but she didn't much care. She had purpose in her life. She had mission and devotion, and it was almost noon. She left smiling. Happy. Like most days. She had not the slightest inkling that it was the last time she'd ever see the place.

> *Delta Dawn,*
> *What's that flower you have on...*

Rose was in her fifties, an old and beaten fifties. Marks of a hard life and many tolls chalked up even before Matt went off to war. The clothes (somewhat dated and therefore oddly current) were worn but clean, and as always, there was a fresh flower. Rose, drowning in depression and despair, somehow managed to bestow good cheer most everywhere she went.

Not all the stories Parker heard actually touched the heart. But Halifax was different and he wanted to hear her story, which she was most anxious to tell. As is often the case, it began with a declaration of her innocence. "I was at a bridal shower, and like everyone else I had a little too much wine and not enough pasta, but I was okay. We're just being girls, talking, laughing, crying, just you know being together."

"Sounds like you're in the clear."

"Right? So this dancer arrives and I admit, I thought wow. It turns out that he wasn't there just to dance and some of the women, one by one, went off with him for a little private time."

"Ah."

"No, not me. Okay, at one point I brushed his cock when he danced up to me."

"Brushed?"

"I held it for a minute. Maybe not that long. Someone yelled let him go and I did. But when they started the parade to the bedroom, I was out of there."

"Probably a good idea."

"Okay, sure, but I'm so turned on I don't know what to do with myself and I thought no, no, I'm taking this home, a gift."

"I don't really need to hear all the..." He took his hand off her shoulder. "You know what? I'm gonna suggest you skip the Special."

"So I'm racing home. Did I mention that my husband is an abusive prick who not only hits me from time to time but loves to put me down in private and in public – and I'm so fucking dependent I'm rushing home to this asshole I never loved in the first place so I can do him like I haven't since our honeymoon—"

"If you don't want to share—"

"But I do. I'm in the right here and I want everyone to know. Especially you."

"Why me?" he tried.

"Cause you knew Rose."

"Not that well."

"So I get home and right there in front of my face, what do I see! I see that micro-putz of a husband on the living room floor with my best friend Libby."

"Ow. Heartbreak. That's something Rose would relate to..."

"I mean I'm standing there just trying to register what I'm seeing. Libby's on her hands and knees and she looks up and sees me and she's about to say something but she can't because she starts coming and screaming and moaning while trying to signal to me that I should give her a chance to explain and I'm just standing there like I'm watching a movie or something and finally she starts to calm down and looks at me and says, Hi."

"Very polite."

"She does have good manners and I will never forgive myself for this, but I looked right back at her and said, Hi."

"So okay, take the Special, decide later about the pie. Let me get that going for you."

"The thing is, I went back to the party."

Everybody was still there. Happy, relaxed, chilling. She went straight to the bedroom, walked in without knocking and found the dancer splayed out on the bed, spent.

"Oh, God, no" he greeted her.

"The dancer? That's who you're in love with?"

"I wouldn't say in love."

"You're leaving your husband."

"That was going to happen anyway."

"Yup."

"Okay," Halifax called out as Parker walked away, "I'll have the pie."

On the day that Rosie went away, the station was closed down and boarded up, just like it had been the day before and would be the day after. The train hadn't stopped here since the plant closed down. Used to have a yardarm for mailbags but dropped that some time ago too, and in spite of that, Rose stood on the platform every day with her suitcase, waiting for the 11:59.

She'd look down the tracks, and there'd be nothing coming.

But she'd wait. Until the church bell sounded noon, she'd wait.

Now this is the part on which the whole town agrees. Convention established for believers and scoffers alike: On that last day, Rose went to the station and was never seen again.

Legend has it, at its most extreme, that a train, a ghost train so to speak, invisible to all but Rose arrived with Matt on board and they rode off together to eternal bliss.

Locals had more practical explanations, none of which accounted for the healing legacy she left behind.

There are cynics and suspicions. But witnesses too, folks who swore they felt the thunder of the train that day, and others who would sooner believe that a long dead soldier had actually returned to life than that a train had stopped here.

"Can I get you another cup?" Parker asked Halifax.

"You work too hard, you know that?" she replied. "You ought to relax a little."

"Be more like my brother? A lot of people still say that."

"You have a brother?"

"Oh," he was surprised she didn't know.

"Had."

"I'm sorry, I didn't mean to—"

"Matt. My brother was married to Rose."

"And got killed in the war!" She did indeed know more but she never made the connection. "You're little Parker. Oh my God!"

"I was."

"And now you're all grown up and working too hard."

"Just padding my pension," he laughed.

She touched his hand. She didn't mean to, it was sort of automatic. "You get old whether you save a single damn penny or not."

He'd have a lot more pennies were it not for Rose. No one asked him to, no one expected him to, but he took on the responsibility of his brother's widow. With a full heart. And never thought of it as a burden though of course she could be one hell of one. Especially when old began creeping into the picture.

"Rose," he ventured once, with difficulty but inspired by the possibility of solution. "I'm right thinking you got no family, that right?"

"You think I might have forgot someone? A sister I don't remember? You took me to my cousin's funeral. That was the last of them. You're the closest thing I got left."

"I didn't mean it like that. How about I fry you a couple over easy, a few strips, some hash browns."

"I guess I might as well get my cholesterol off your griddle as anywhere else," Rose relented.

"You do need to eat regular," he said, "you heard the social worker."

"Damn, Parker! Is that what this is about?"

The visit had not gone well. Rose thought the young woman was impudent, irrelevant and had no business prying. The woman couldn't get a real answer out of her.

"Could I ask you a few questions about how you're doing?"

Rose sang to her. *"Delta Dawn, what's that flower you have on ..."*

"I can't help you," the woman pleaded, "if you don't help me."

"I guess we're done, then."

"No Rose, we're not."

"Take you to his mansion in the sky," she sang.

"Stop playing with me. I have to make an official report about you. I know you're not crazy, so please..."

"Thank you," Rose said. Most people thought she was in very deep denial, but that's just because they didn't understand. She wasn't trying to deny anything. She was trying to change it. Make it so it never happened.

But denial? There was none of that. Every night, without fail, it came to her. And every night she replayed the story. Every night she tried to climb into the dream and save him. Lose herself if she had to, but save him. And every night, she failed.

So crazy, a little, yes, how could you not be when your world falls away. If she let it go now, it would be like killing him.

So every night she dreams it. Every night. She sees it.

Matt's team is pinned down. In real life fourteen hours, an instant in the dream. They eventually shoot their way out and avoid catastrophe. She dreams that Matt is a key factor because he'd al-ways been a good shot.

The men wander back to town to celebrate. Spent and sleep-deprived it wasn't going to be much of a celebration. More of a token we-didn't-die-today res-ignation. Surviving can often be more stressful than the combat, like extended versions of the lulls be-tween barrages.

Slogging home they pass a house on fire. Not a combat casualty, but burning just as hot. Flame and smoke fail to muffle the screams from inside.

Matt turns to the fire. Sarge grabs him. "What the fuck you doing!"

"There's people in there!"

"Not our people."

"People," Matt explains, and shakes him off. He drops his gear and runs for the house.

Matt saves two children and a badly wounded man, and when he goes back in for a third time, the entire building implodes and he becomes part of the raging flame.

The inferno burns so hot, they never find a body to send home.

"They'll put you in some loony bin cause they think you can't take care of yourself anymore," Parker scolded, trying not to raise his voice.

"That's ridiculous. You know I can take care of myself."

"A month ago you took your clothes off in the fountain!"

"They were fixing my shower! I explained!"

"And before that you were getting your stomach pumped because you took six of your damn pills every hour instead of one every six hours."

"Everyone gets a little absent-minded now and—"

"It's one thing to be forgetful, but they're saying you're not connected to reality and they want to put you somewhere and sit you in a chair so you can stare at the walls all day."

"Not me, I'm going to the lake when my time comes."

The mere mention of the lake made her blush and sent her off to familiar reverie.

She and Matt would just lie on the grass and talk about exactly where to put the house. Which way the bedroom should face so the sun didn't grab them too early, and where the kitchen should be for those grand views of the valley.

They never got around to it. The war came too fast and the best they could manage was an on the fly Justice of the Peace wedding and a surplus army tent they lived in for two glorious weeks before he was called up.

They hiked up rugged mountain trails where they would most certainly be alone. They picked berries, and fried war surplus meal packs they thought were delicious because they were in love and all they really cared about was crawling into each other's soul and fucking their brains out.

And eating. "We baked our own bread up there," she reminded Parker.

The Army tent was way bigger than they'd imagined and impossible to keep warm, unless you got very close. And they did. They practically became each other.

"No social worker and no judge," Rose assured Parker, "can take that away from me."

"Yes they can."

"I have to go, I don't want to be late."

He finally said it. For years he managed to sub-due reality in favor of comforting Rose, and then it just came blurting out. "Rose, there is no train."

It stunned her for a moment. Him too.

"What do you mean?"

"I mean there is no train."

Rose took it well. She had perspective after all. "It was the storm wasn't it? Knocked the bridge out up in Tremont? Not the first time."

"No, it's not about—"

"They usually get it fixed in a day or two."

"Rose, it has nothing to do with the bridge."

"What then?"

"There is no train. There hasn't been a train here since I was a kid."

She stared at him, panicked and frightened. "What do you mean?"

"There's no train, Rose."

"Why are you saying that!"

He knew immediately that he had done some-thing terrible. She was right. She lived in the world she lived in, and it suited her. Who was he to burst anyone's bubble.

"It's not me," he said reversing course, "it's the damn train people. Somebody oughta do something about it."

"My goodness, is that what you think? There goes crazy old Rosie, looking for a train that's never coming?"

"No, of course not."

"Why not, the rest of the town does?"

"No. No one..."

"Matt always said I had a screw loose."

"I remember. 'How could a beauty like her love a farm boy like me less she had a screw loose.'"

She laughed. "I used to love to listen to him talk. Didn't much matter what he was saying. God, I miss hearing him talk. I'm so confused sometimes I don't know what's real and what's not anymore."

"Sounds like the rest of us."

"Matt's real, isn't he?" she pleaded.

"Oh, Rose." Swamped by her agony it was all he could manage.

"Matt's real, yes? I didn't make that up."

In all the years since Rose has been gone, Parker never told this story to anyone. He didn't understand why he gave it all to Halifax, or why she listened.

"You did a generous and loving thing," she assured him.

Then it got a little close and clumsy. He gave her directions to where Rose's house used to be, and how to get to the Station from there. He warned her that the station was hardly worth the trip and not to get her hopes up.

They shook hands and said goodbye.

He waved when she looked back and he felt that empty clutch in his belly when she disappeared around the corner and evaporated from his life.

Rose lived in a small house, encumbered by too much of everything. Too much furniture, too much hanging on the walls, too many piles of old memories, some so well-forgotten they didn't even disturb her anymore.

In the bedroom, on the dresser, she maintained what amounts to an altar to Matt. It's not ornate or overdone, but an altar all the same. It was for Rose the physical evidence that he would return.

There was a gilt-framed photo of him in uniform. Very young and handsome, and a photo album and two candles that she lit at bedtime.

Just long enough to whisper, "I love you," and hang out a bit.

Nights were never good to her. It was the loneliest time.

Halifax could feel the lonely desperation when she stood out front where the house used to be. She watched people leave flowers for Rose – no need to explain what kind. And not just broken-heart basket cases like herself, she noticed, but local folks too who still miss her, and remember.

They leave flowers and beseech to be heard.

"Rose," seekers who never knew her whispered intimately as they lay their offerings on the ground. "Rose, I don't want to bother you but..."

"Rose, oh God Rose I am so screwed."

"I can't have this baby, Rose. I just can't."

"Rose, oh Rose. Oh Rose. Oh. Oh. Rose."

No one left untouched. She answered every one but Halifax, or so it seemed to her. She had promised herself that she wasn't going to ask for anything, but couldn't stop herself from thinking it: "How do I know true love?"

She heard nothing. Received no revelation.

The train station was as advertised. Tightly shuttered. Hardly worth the walk. Parker was right. There was nothing here. Until for reasons uncertain, she found herself waiting for the train. Filling up with anxiety and anticipation. She peered down the track.

This all happened in the blink of an eye and Halifax never could explain it anyway, but suddenly, there was Rose!

A much younger Rose, wearing finer, newer clothes. She was the blushing bride waiting for the love of her life to arrive on the 11:59.

Halifax didn't move. She thought she must be hallucinating, but she wasn't imagining anything, or seeing anything. She just felt it.

Halifax couldn't answer for what was happening, but she trembled with anticipation when she heard the train.

It billowed enormous clouds of steam, seeding the heavens.

She heard Rose laugh.

She felt the heat of the train along with the lumbering rumble of its enormous load.

It spewed smoke and flame. And then it stopped. The damn train stopped. The magic of love unyielding delivered on its promise. He came home.

> *And did I hear you say*
> *He'd be meeting you here today*
> *To take you*
> *To his mansion in the sky*

Matt stepped from the train, as young and handsome as everyone remembered.

> *Delta Dawn, what's that flower you have on?*

Rose couldn't move.

The answer of a lifetime stood before her.

"I am so sorry to have kept you waiting," he said.

Rose cried out. An agony of release. "Not at all."

"I love you, Rose," he said and picked her up and carried her onto the train.

It all happened in less than a blink, but Halifax saw it. She saw the spark, she saw the answer. Halifax waved as the train pulled out. Love's easy, that's how you know. "Thank you," she called out. "Thank you."

Parker was shutting down when Halifax returned. His heart soared and he thought, Rose, I owe you one. He meant to say how glad he was to see her but it came out all wrong. "Sorry," he said, "but I'm closed down."

"Not as much as you think."

"Right," he said missing the point, "I could fix you a sandwich."

There were still tables to clear, and brooming for sure. "I can help you finish up," she offered, clearing the table closest to her.

"You don't have to do that."

"I spoke to Rose today," she said.

"And she told you I needed help here?"

"She never said a word—"

He was relieved to hear that. He had no problem with anyone talking to Rose, hell he did it all the time, but he couldn't bear reports from people who heard her talking back.

"But she taught me what I needed to know."

"Trust your heart?"

"Well, first know your heart."

"Know your heart?"

"They're tricky little bastards, hearts," she explained, "and they'll trip you up every which way to

68

Sunday. Make you think you're in love when it's just a cardiac fart, or send you chasing after empty promises."

Been there, done that, he thought.

"The heart," she told him, and she was speaking from personal experience, "your heart will lie to you directly. To your face, but only because it wants to see you happy."

He was lulled by the sounds, just glad to be with her.

"Love," she said winding up, "is easy."

"Rose teach you that?"

"No, you did," she told him. Men are just blind, she thought, because they only have the two eyes.

"That's not what I see around here."

"Love is easy. Relationships are hard," she said, "which is why I think we should start slowly."

"Could you please put the dishes down."

"I'm just going to stack them in the sink."

"Start what slowly?"

"Our life together," she said, surprised he hadn't caught up to her yet, "what do you mean?"

"We hardly even know each other."

"Isn't that exciting. It will never be this easy again. For either of us. So..."

"And this is slow enough for you?"

"Yes," she said, "yes it is."

So Parker did something he hadn't done for a very long time. He locked the doors, and pulled the shades.

He said something as he walked back to her but she couldn't quite make it out.

"What was that?" she asked.

"You wash," he said, "I'll dry."

— ◊ —

LITTLE JEFFY'S PENIS

"I hate her!"

"How many times do I have to tell you not to slam the door?"

"I don't know." She didn't even know how many times she'd been told. She knew only that it hadn't taken hold yet and had no idea how much longer before it would, if it actually did. On the other hand, the sentiment without the slam would have been a little feeble. Not significant enough to merit the blooming fury to which she felt entitled.

"It wasn't a question," Mom called back from the kitchen where she was repairing a door hinge, "and leave your backpack on the stairs."

Yet another instruction not quite fully absorbed. It had been a hard enough day, cooped up in a classroom for God knows how long – which they themselves weren't expected to know until next year. First grade is not the romp one might anticipate, kindergarten it is not. It's tough. Something new every day. Every day.

"How was school?"

"I learned how much six plus six is."

"That's exciting."

"Yup."

"How much is it?"

"I don't remember."

"Twelve?"

"Maybe. Mom, how can you tell if someone's a boy or a girl?"

"You're six years old, you know who's a boy and who's a girl."

"No, I don't. Not all the time."

"Well, what about Cheryl?"

"I hate her."

"I thought she was your best friend."

"Uh-huh."

"Is she a boy or a girl?"

"Cheryl? She's a girl."

"How do you know that?

"She told me."

"That's it? She told you?"

"Well she doesn't pick her nose and eat it like boys do. And she has a cat."

"I saw Lisa do it. Does that make her a boy?"

"No."

"How come?"

"She has a vagina and she vaginates with it. Like me."

"Urinates."

"That's funny. That's what Teacher calls it too."

"It's just a word. It'll stop being funny around freshman year of High School. Could you please hand me that screwdriver. The yellow one."

"Urinate? Urinate. No, Mom, it is funny."

"Okay, but being a girl is about a lot more than having a vagina."

"Jeffy's not a girl."

"Jeffy?"

"From Tae Kwan Do? He wore eye make-up? And I hated him?"

"Jeffy. Of course."

"His mother lets him wear make-up if he wants to."

"I know."

"So, I—"

"No. No makeup."

"Do you want everyone to think he has a better mom than me?"

"Anyone but you."

"It's not fair. How come boys can wear makeup and I can't?"

"I didn't say that."

"You're mean."

"Why?"

"Because I like him."

"I thought you hated him. "

"Last year, but look at him now, Mom. He's gorgeous."

"Gorgeous? That's a lot of liking."

"We're getting married."

"Congratulations. He asked you to marry him?"

"No, I told him."

"How did this romance blossom so suddenly."

"He showed me his penis."

"Um...what did you say?" She knew perfectly well, and as a stalling tactic it had a very short half-life. She did not immediately embrace the notion that oh well kids are kids and this natural curiosity was not only healthy, it was necessary. Nope, she went immediately to Local News disaster. Scandal. Shame. Humiliation. Changing schools. Broken psyches.

"He showed me his penis."

"I know. I heard you." But it wasn't all she heard. She heard McMartin, where lives were destroyed by a few lies and a handful of hysterical parents. She heard U Penn, where it was all true. She heard talk of the local seminary. She heard a tidal onslaught coiling to strike.

Be a mother, she told herself. Don't panic. Don't let her see you're already in panic mode. "He showed you his penis?

"Teacher told him to."

There you have it. She did not gasp out loud. Whatever trauma may have occurred, or not, she was determined not to add to it. Be gentle, she kept thinking. Be gentle. The wrong words now, the wrong curl of her lip or flex of an eyebrow could have permanent and devastating repercussions for this beautiful little child for years to come.

"Evelyn told him to show you his penis?" she asked as if inquiring about a homework assignment.

"Not exactly." She was tired of talking and just wanted to get out and run and laugh where there weren't any doors not to slam.

Mom was sad. The world had changed. When she herself was a child, playing doctor and other curiosities, it seemed no big deal. If you were caught you were told to go out and play. Now, the most natural of explorations is greeted with outright panic.

It wasn't little Jeffy's penis or her daughter's interest that scared her, it was the stigmas that were now attached to it. Some mother would hear of it and whisper to another and before you know it some childish hanky panky has become a neighborhood witch hunt.

"Can we just sit down here for a minute. Thank you." She left the tools on the counter and pulled a chair up to the table. Only she sat. First things first, get the facts right. "Are you saying that Evelyn told Jeffy to show you his penis?"

"Uh-huh."

"What did she say exactly?"

"She said, Jeffy, I told you not to wear a dress to class today."

"He was wearing a dress?

"He said he could run faster."

"And because he was wearing a dress Evelyn ...um...?"

"Evelyn what?"

"No, that's what I'm asking you. What did Evelyn do."

"She said he had to go home and change and then she went out and came back in to get her phone and then she went out again and then Jeffy's Mom came and yelled at her."

"Yelled at her?"

"Not yelling yelling, just with her finger."

"Her finger?"

"Like you do when cars don't stop for us to cross the street. And then Teacher cried and said Jeffy could stay and he could wear whatever he wanted but he didn't want to so he went to the cloakroom because he was sad."

"And you went to the cloakroom so he wouldn't be alone?"

"He was very sad."

"And that's where it happened?"

"What happened?"

"Yes, what happened?"

"I told him to stop crying."

"Very comforting of you."

"I said Jeffy stop crying right this minute. Just stop it."

"I see."

"And I gave him the band-aid from my backpack."

"Your band-aid? With the stars?

"It was an emergency and I remember you told me to take the band-aid for an emergency."

"You are something else."

"What am I?"

"I mean, you're wonderful and I love you."

"He put the band-aid on like a moustache and he felt better. We laughed and I asked him if he was a boy or a girl."

"Just like that?"

"That's something I should know if I'm going to marry him."

"Absolutely."

"Then Mrs. Uberfeldt came to talk to Teacher and burned her and she started crying and—"

"Burned her?"

"No?"

"Burned like fire!?"

"That's it, fired her."

"Oh my God." It was too late. She had to call Uberfeldt, no better in person, and nip this in the bud.

"What does it mean?"

"It means Evelyn is not going to be your teacher anymore." It means this is going public and they are all screwed.

"But I want her to."

"Sweetheart, what happened in the cloakroom?"

I told Jeffy we couldn't get married if I didn't know if he was a boy or a girl."

"And then?"

"He lifted up his dress and showed me his penis. He's a boy."

"Oh." Say the wrong thing now and screw up the kid forever. Sex. Romance. Therapy. Drummer. Rehab. No no no no no. "Oh," she repeated.

"It was little. I don't know how he could get a baby through it but he said it was only little because we were six but that it would get much, much bigger. "

"They all say that."

"Is that true?"

"What?"

"That it will get big enough to get a baby through it?"

"That's not how it works, exactly." She could handle this. Biology. Piece of cake, biology.

"Oh yes it is, the man gives the wife a baby. We saw the book."

"Did Evelyn know you were in the cloakroom?"

"We were hiding."

Hiding. A word she definitely didn't want to hear. Hiding is rife with implicit possibilities. Easy to misconstrue. All it takes is one crazy sex-freaked mom to lose it and the next thing you know you show up on the nightly news as *that woman*. Jeffy is branded forever as a deviant, and her own daughter faces a sexually stunted life all because of her, because she doesn't know what to do to keep this all private and under wraps.

"And after he showed you his penis, what happened."

"Cheryl took the apple."

"What apple?"

"Teacher got everything from her desk, but left her apple and Cheryl just took it."

"I want to know about the penis." It felt like someone else, someone she didn't know – maybe her mother – was speaking in her mouth.

"I thought you knew about them."

"I want to know about Jeffy's penis!" Words she never ever imagined saying, especially in that tone of voice. She immediately regretted it and instantly suspected hidden cameras everywhere recording it. She knew then and there that keeping it together was not going to be easy. Just stay calm and act like you're not freaking about some little boy's penis, she reasoned. This does not have to turn into an unmitigated calamity.

"I didn't see it much. He showed it to me and then he went out to play kickball."

"Nothing else happened?"

"Like what?"

"Oh...I don't know."

"Mom."

"Like...touching?"

"Touching what?"

"Jeffy."

"I touch him a lot but mostly I just push him or kick him. Sometimes I knock him down."

"His penis. Did you touch—"

"Eww. You're gross."

"Thank you God."

"Why?"

"Because sometimes things like this can get out of hand and cause trouble. Lots and lots of trouble."

"How come?"

"Because some people forget how curious they were as kids and they misunderstand, so it's better not to mention this to anyone because we don't want it to blossom into some suburban crusade that ends with us all going to jail."

"What about Cheryl? Can't she go to jail? I told her. Don't take that apple."

"I don't think so. I'm being a little hyperbolic."

"Does that mean you need to breathe into a bag?"

"Thank you, no, I'm fine."

"You don't look fine, Mom."

"So there was no touching, is that right?"

"Not until the wedding."

"Exactly."

"Or whenever it gets big enough."

"So it sounds to me like you're fine, yes?"

"What do you mean?"

"It didn't scare you or—"

"Mom, it's this little wrinkly thing. He said it gets straight when he tickles it so he tried to but it didn't. You can hardly see it in the picture unless you pinch it up."

"You took a picture?"

"Sure."

"Oh God."

"What?"

"No, just whispering to myself."

"You're telling yourself a secret?"

"You mind if I just look at your phone for a min— No. What I do not want to look at is your phone and invade your privacy."

"I have a privacy?"

"What I mean is that I'd like you to erase the picture from your phone before—"

"Okay."

"Oh. Okay." It took all of a second and a half and just felt too damn easy. "Just one picture, Honey?"

"Uh-huh. Wait. Okay. It's gone."

"Thank you. Okay, listen carefully. You can't talk to anyone else about this. Just me. And I'm just going to talk to Jeffy's Mom and Uberfeldt, but nobody else."

"How come?"

"Because we don't want Mrs. Uberfeldt to say bad things in his file that might make some people think they don't like Jeffy."

"She's a poopy head. Everybody likes Jeffy."

"So you understand? We can't talk about this for a while except to each other, and maybe, just maybe we can get Evelyn back."

"I love you, Mommy."

"I love you too Honeybear. Now go out and play. Chase the dog for a while."

Inside she felt an enormous sigh of grateful relief, confident they could keep this light and silly and private. Laugh about it.

Better for everyone concerned.

Kid was half way out the door when she remembered. "Mom?" she called back, "do you also want me to delete Jeffy's picture from your Facebook page?"

A BREACH AT THE GATES

So this guy arrives at the Pearly Gates and is seen not by the Entry Conductors, nor even by the Level Managers, but by St. Peter himself, royally pissed.

"How did you get here!?"

"I'm not sure. I was cutting someone's throat when I take a bullet to the back of the head." He touches the back of his head to see if there is any sign of the wound, but there is not. "It was his wife, I think."

Peter is not amused. "I know how you died. And worse, I know how you lived."

"What the fuck is that supposed to mean!" Bob's shock is genuine. Everyone watching can see that it is genuine. He wasn't a polished man, but he wasn't stupid. St. Peter himself was telling him that he didn't belong in Heaven and he was deeply offended.

"You," Peter said, looking for a euphemism for miserable bag of shit, "are an evil man."

"I am shocked. If I still had breath I would say it takes my fucking breath away. Why the fuck should I be barred!? Evil man! What the fuck are you talking about! God loves me!"

Now, Peter is a busy guy. It's not like the old days when you could pretty much welcome everybody personally. Now it's all he can do to keep up with the Popes and the high and the mighty, and the holy, and every now and then it was his great pleasure to meet one of the truly humble. So, how was he to find the time to dicker with a man like this. And why? It would be nice if someone told him why. "Do we really need to have this conversation, Bob?"

"Yes." Bob knew not everybody liked him. "I'm pleading for my eternal soul, here." And he knew that his style of life wasn't everybody's teacup, but Christ, he thought, whose is?

Peter was patient. Gentle Peter. Gentle, busy, pissed off Peter. The saint. "Are you just plain nuts!"

"I'm desperate."

"You are a horrible excuse for a human being. You cheated and robbed and twisted people your entire life. You murdered four people!"

"It was manslaughter. They could never prove murder."

"Prove? Do you understand who you're talking to?"

"All that's behind me now," Bob explained.

"Because you're dead? That's not how it works."

"I gave to charity. I supported my church. I loved and protected my family."

"You killed thirteen people!"

"Nine at war. That doesn't count."

"Of course it does.

"And the four you killed when you got back, that doesn't count either?"

"I prayed for every one of them."

"No you didn't."

"I thought about it."

"Counts for shit."

"Excuse me?"

"Excrement."

"You have no right to bar me from Heaven."

"Of course I do, I'm the Guardian of the Gates."

"Only God can deny me his presence."

"Excuse me?"

"Only God."

Peter was stymied. All these years as a prime deputy and no one, no one ever challenged his authority before.

"You were appointed to guide people in," Bob explained, "not bar them."

"The choice is mine," Peter argued, knowing full well the man was right.

"I did what I was created to do."

"You're not making any friends."

"I'm not looking for friends. I want to know why I lived my life the way I did."

"Because you chose to."

"I haven't lived a single night without terrifying nightmares. You think I chose that!"

"You were given free will."

"Bullshit. I was given a smorgasbord of choices, all of it defined and limited by what was on the table, by the constraints of my own understanding."

"Exactly."

"And the limits of my understanding were pre-scribed by God. God made the rules, I followed what he put in my heart."

"No, no, no. God gave you Free Will."

"Absolutely, and I used it."

"You don't understand. Having free will means the ability to do the right thing."

"Exactly."

"So..."

"I did what God put in my heart. I prayed. I asked him to change my mind. For weeks before I killed the pregnant woman. God, no. Please don't ask this of me. When he didn't answer I knew I had to obey His will."

"It was not God's will that you kill her!"

"Then why did it happen?!

"Because you threw a rope around her neck and choked the life out of her."

"Because He wanted me to."

"God did not want you to."

"Then why didn't he stop me?"

"Free will. You were supposed to stop you."

"I don't think you understand what free will means."

"I'm Saint Peter, I don't understand!?"

"Could we just agree to disagree?"

"Those voices in your head are not God."

"What?"

"Not God. He was not talking to you."

"I heard Him."

"Wasn't Him. You know how I know? Because he hardly ever, ever speaks to anybody. Anybody."

"That's not true, I know lots of—"

"Anybody."

"I think we have an impasse here. I'd like to speak to your Supervisor."

With centuries of practice, Peter was a pretty un-flappable guy, but Bob hit a button that had never been hit before. "Go to Hell!"

"No."

"Go to Hell."

"I got to hear it from God."

"Bob? Hey," a Voice called out. Peter was aghast, God hardly ever came to the Gates.

"Hey," Bob answered.

"Just wanted to say," God said, "I'm sorry about the life I put you through but it was necessary and you were the only one I could count on to do it. But you're home now and that's what counts."

"Amen," Bob said.

"Does this mean," Peter asked, "that I should let him in?"

God laughed. A big hearty rattle-the-heavens laugh. "Should I let him in?" he parroted, mocking Peter and hurting his feelings.

"Look at that," Bob said when he was sure God was nowhere around, "you can hear the voices in my head too."

Saint Peter said fuck you and wrote Bob's name in the Book.

Heaven is a small place, but Bob and Peter rarely ran into each other, for which they both thanked God – but only Bob wrote an actual note.

DOC AND THE BUNGALOW
QUEEN

1.

In Santa Monica, on a quiet street just blocks from the beach, I came across a story engraved in cement. Not the whole story – no beginning, middle or end – just the hook.

Doc and the Bungalow Queen.

That's all it says.

I had no idea what it meant and I was fairly confident I never would, not for sure. But it was magical. Mysterious.

This was a marker about a love soaring so high that it had to be a celebration. *Doc and the Bungalow Queen*. In orbit. Somewhere. This old concrete note was a song of love, elevated and perhaps ecstatic. A simple phrase that radiated a love so pure it could inspire the world. Maybe even cure it.

It said so right there on the sidewalk. Love is the answer.

I stared in wonder. It was what we've hoped for a thousand generations – love is true, love is real, love is the answer.

As I stood there contemplating the wonderful fantasy of human beings actually rising to the ideals of love, the sky inside began to darken. I found myself looking at the very same words and they bore only pain.

I began to sense that this was no declaration of joy, but a sad and bitter farewell Doc had scrawled on the day he left. I felt suddenly witness to the utter shock and bewilderment of a protest hastily chiseled. They were breaking up. Doc was in agony, and he left it etched in stone: You and me. What more can a man say on city property? This was piss-marking straight from his tortured heart.

I figured Doc was in a state of shock and denial about the split and this was the closest he could come to saying I love you. He couldn't believe this was happening and dug the words in protest. It wasn't a perfect job and it caused one to think Doc was no surgeon. Perhaps not even a Doc type Doc.

Maybe he was a card player with a penchant for cheating. Doctoring the cards. Or dice. And that's why she threw him out. She just couldn't take it any-more.

The gambler's life is not for everyone. The con-stant travel, like vagabonds, and trying to keep track of who you are or why you are or what the hell are you doing in a country club – other than the massages and the towel boy.

Well, there go dreams. Love is just long-term graf-fiti. I had to get out of there.

2.

It was weeks before I walked that way, not entirely by accident. I was haunted by it. Maybe I'd been wrong. Too hard on Doc. Maybe there was more to this sidewalk than meets the eye.

And there was. Bathed in sunlight, the inscription heralded a hopeful beginning. Kids maybe. For sure an addition to the house, kids or not.

Good. Fine. I left before the clouds moved in.

They caught up with me about four in the morn-ing. Woke me. She was having an affair!?

Was that what this was all about? Revenge? Doc had a long resume of earned points, any one of which could have set her on the path of exquisitely sordid sex on soft white towels with the uncompromising thrill that someone might walk in on them. Not hard to see why he'd be upset, still, you don't go around posting ownership declarations. She's not property.

Doc and the Bungalow Queen.

Not an accusation to be permanently etched on the street.

3.

Maybe it wasn't that at all. Maybe she was called Queen because she owned all the bungalows on the block. Or sold bungalows for a living and was very good at it. Or she was the most beautiful woman in the neighborhood?

Even though people walk on it instead of around like they might with, say the Lincoln Memorial, the inscription is a monument not a tombstone.

Unless he killed her. Holy shit, was the imprint a confession!? Is good so thinly veiled from evil that a celebration in cement could be read as its very own opposite.

But why! He loved her. Is passion so febrile it can flip from insatiable hunger to murderous rage without noticing? Doc loves the Bungalow Queen. Doc kills the Bungalow Queen. Doc and the Bungalow Queen. Now immutable but still mortal. Some day the sidewalk will get repaved and that will be the end of that. Doc will be forgotten. The Queen will be forgotten. And the meaning of the *and* will be lost forever.

Worried that I might forget the awesome curiosity of this chiseled message, I got my phone out and took pictures. I also found myself in a variety of embarrassing contortions trying to get me into the shot. A selfie stick would have helped.

I was looking upside down through my legs and felt like a complete idiot when I saw the little old lady hauling some groceries down the street on her cart. She seemed amused by my efforts to straighten up and recover some semblance of dignity.

Well into her nineties she carried herself with undiminished grace. She was proud and bold and radiant. And I seemed to amuse her. Like a two-year old might.

I chose, unwisely, to address my own discomfort by engaging her. Generously. Cheerfully. "Hi, do you know anything about this?"

"About what?"

"Doc and the Bungalow Queen," I pointed out.

"I didn't do it," she told him, "I can tell you that."

"It's been here a while though, I'm guessing."

"I moved here when I was seven and it's been here since then," she explained. "That'd make it almost eighty-five years."

"Here?" he was thrilled. "In this very bungalow?"

"Why would anyone want to move from here?" She had no more time for idle gossip and was anxious to be home.

"And you're sure you don't know anything?"

"I did hear that they lived happily ever after, if that's what you need to know."

That was it exactly and I was grateful.

4.

The old woman watched the young man walk away. He was not the first to stumble over that silly sidewalk. For years she'd watched people do just that, and to be fair, it really annoyed her.

Fumbling with her keys at the front door, she dropped them twice. Sometimes these days when she dropped things, she'd get angry about it – the betrayal of the body – but this time she just shrugged it off.

This time, instead of feeling like a clumsy old fool, she was excited and nervous, like a young woman using her lover's key for the very first time. She was happy even before she got the door unlocked.

"Your Majesty," he called out from the kitchen, "I've missed you."

"You oughta do something about that sidewalk. I think it's making people a little crazy."

"Let 'em cross the street or walk somewhere else. That thing is sacred to people and I'm not messing with it."

"It's not sacred."

"It's not our sidewalk and you are not calling the City. Period," he commanded before he took a breath and added, "Please?"

"What about the porch then, it needs painting," she reminded him, "or is that too holy too?"

He laughed. Old and creaky as they'd become, they still laughed.

"You ever wonder about it yourself?" he asked.

"About Doc and the Bungalow Queen?"

"Yes, who else we talking about?"

"No."

"No? You never wonder who they were?"

"I've thought about it, I suppose."

"Didn't you wonder what it meant? What happened to them? C'mon."

"I'm not a fan of gossip and I don't pry into the private affairs of other people," she announced, putting an end to the discussion.

"Oh my God!" He was ninety-three years old. He had spent virtually his entire life with this woman, and this was the first time he realized that he was Doc!

"Oh my God!" she whispered, absolutely thrilled to know that she had successfully kept this secret all her life. And she felt a tiny bit guilty. But not so guilty that she was going to feel bad about it. Or in fact, even admit it. "And what, I'm a queen? You call me that because of the damn sidewalk, not the other way around."

"I..." he said. They have been together for so long it was sometimes difficult to know if the cart came before the horse or after it. She was probably right, he thought, she has a better memory for these things than I do. And a moment later he thought, what?

She wasn't going to let a few more lies spoil her record now. "Whoever they are and wherever they are, I wish for them what we have."

"The diabetes or the arthritis?"

She walked over and kissed him. "The joy. The connection."

"You're right. I'm sure they'd rather have that."

And with a knowing groan, they moved on. She sat close to him on the sofa and held his hand and watched the flaming display in the fireplace. She was exactly where, at the age of seven, she dreamed she'd be if everything worked out.

They had just moved into the neighborhood. The carters were still hauling stuff into the house when she spotted the boy across the street and couldn't take her eyes off him. "Mom," she demanded full of life-affirming excitement, "I want to meet my husband."

"You may have to wait a little while for that."

"How long?"

"Years probably."

"Could you at least tell me his name?"

"I...I don't know his name."

"Could you ask his mother? He lives across the street." It didn't really matter. She'd already decided.

He would become a doctor and she would become a queen, and that's what she carved into the still somewhat wet cement.

Eighty-five years later, holding his hand by the fire, she felt what she felt the first time she saw him, and she blushed.

5.

It was a couple of years before I passed that way again and it is true, there is only once. You can stand in the same spot, think the same things and finally figure out that what's changed is you.

I don't know why it had been so long, or what brought me back on that particular day. I'd like to think it was some ethereal pull, some mystical connection, but I' pretty sure it was just happenstance, like the first time.

Sometimes a touchstone is invested with too much. The symbol becomes the thing, and we are crushed by its destruction. I round the corner and panic when I see the FOR SALE sign dangling from its post.

I walk faster. It doesn't help.

The place was empty and three or four guys were working on it. A quick appraisal made it clear that this was going to be way more than a paint job. I must have been staring because one of them came out and said yo Dude wassup, and we bumped and I asked him what the fuck and gestured to the engraving in the sidewalk.

"My aunt," he said.

"Your aunt?"

"Great aunt, I guess. Great-great maybe, she was real old."

"Sorry to hear that."

"No, once Doc was gone, she was done."

There it was. All the confirmation I needed. Mystery solved and I wasn't sure I was the better for it.

"Doc called me," the Dude said, "the thing is I would go by a few times a week, see if they needed anything, which they hardly ever did, and I'd always bring Doc a bran muffin and a hot chocolate from this coffee place he liked."

"You think he carved it?"

"Nobody knows. So Doc calls me and says don't bother with the muffin, won't need it, I think I'm going to die today."

"Jesus," I mutter.

"No, he wasn't any kind of religious."

"No, I just meant—"

"So I go racing over there and sure enough Doc is out back all bundled up on the porch swing and looking like...I dunno, wasted. Expired. I said, Dudes, we got to get him to a hospital and they both shushed me."

"You're not here to help me," Doc told him, "you're here to help her."

"You can't die, you old porcupine," she admonished, "the devil doesn't want you and heaven won't take you so you're stuck here with me."

"I can tell you Your Majesty, with absolute confidence, that there is no other place I'd rather be."

"Don't die, you bastard, don't die."

He reached out and found her hand. "You are my heart," he said.

"Please," she said, "no."

He laughed.

"What?

"I took your virginity."

"Oh, was that you?"

He laughed again, and coughed a little. The light grew dim, and he was colder even under all the blankets. He looked into her eyes and said, "You are the best woman a man ever had."

"That's sexist!" she accused, fighting hard not to burst into tears. "Do not leave me."

"Best friend, best partner, best liar," he whispered.

"It's just a stupid drawing in the sidewalk."

"Thank you," he said, "and I love you anyway."

"Couple of months later," the Dude explained, "she was gone too. That's how come I got the place."

Not long after the renovation was complete and he moved in, I drove by. The place looked great. Like it must once have.

There was a bronze plaque on display. It said simply:

> *Doc and the Bungalow Queen*
> *were here.*

And I remember them.

— ◊ —

KATY BY THE KESTREL

They saw a kestrel. Jack and Katy, when the day started to cool.

They were bouldering and the bird flew within inches of her face and hovered there. Staring at her, locking into her eyes. It's feathers shimmered in kaleidoscopic brilliance and its eyes pierced every survival tactic she had ever devised.

It was the first time in her life that she had ever experienced being the object of a predator's attention. It is a predicament for most creatures only once in a lifetime, and it is shrouded in perfect clarity. There are only two options, life and death. In either case, it's a defining moment.

In her head she knew this bird couldn't kill her, in her head she was calm and brave and even displayed a little attitude, but the rest of her was terrified, and she froze.

She was no deer and there were no headlights, but she froze. The kestrel is a very small hawk, but its intentions were clear. It seemed only to be trying to figure out how to carry off something that size.

She felt like she was staring death directly in the eyes. She was absolutely trapped, and fully exposed. She couldn't move, and surrendered to her fate. She felt her stomach turn and her knees wobble.

In a moment it was over. The kestrel was gone as quickly as it had arrived, and she breathed, and blinked, and then she laughed, born back into the world. She laughed again when she realized how excited and wet she was.

Eros trumps Thanatos. Or is. The line is clearly more blurred than we like to consider. The abject terror of death becomes the engine of re-birth, and fucking the heartbeat of immortality.

Back in the car, she couldn't stop smiling and occasionally giggling. She could not have felt more triumphant. She was the gazelle besting a lion, the paratrooper whose chute finally did open. She was excited and hungry and reached into his lap.

"I should take you hiking more often," he encouraged.

"It's the trees, the smell of the trees," she said because it was too embarrassing to own up to the kestrel. "Take me to the trees more often."

She leaned in closer. Her hand continued to work his lap and it was too intense to ignore.

"Kate...I...we're on the Freeway...Katherine—"

"Not my problem, I'm not driving," she explained, thrilled with her control.

"Katherine, seriously, we can't..."

"You're saying no?!"

"I'm saying let's wait 'til we get home."

"When did you get bashful?"

"I'm practicing safe sex by keeping my eyes on the road."

"Okay, you deal with your eyes, I'll take care of the rest."

She unzipped his fly.

"Jesus, Katy, you can't—"

Her head disappeared into his lap and inspired by desire not safety, he immediately cut across two lanes and pulled off to the fortunately broad shoulder.

A short while later there was a knock on the window.

A cop. Highway Patrol.

They burst out laughing. Both of them.

Not Katy.

Life itself however is not quite as simple as fuck or die. Even mythically, there are complications. You figure, from Thanatos to Eros is an easy lay-up, except you run into Civilization, smiling. Civilization is designed to curb unbridled lust.

It doesn't work.

They made it home in record time. Jack came through the door unbuttoning his shirt. A man mid-mission.

Katy was a few steps behind and slammed the door too loudly.

It didn't feel at all like Eros racing to reclaim her. It felt much more like real life.

It stopped him in his tracks. "What did I do?"

She stepped around him on her way to the shower. "You expect me to be in the mood? After what you did?"

She turned on the shower and came back out to undress for it.

"I cut across a couple of lanes of traffic. That's hardly a no-fuck offense."

"You told the cop it was an emergency!"

He was still thrilled to have come up with it. It made the cop laugh. Usually people lie – no sir I know it might have looked like that as you were driving by but she was not... and the ever-popular eighty? No way My speedometer was showing seventy-one miles an hour ask my wife – so when Jack came up with the truth, the cop was very impressed and let them off with a warning: use a condom.

"I was never so embarrassed in my life."

"He laughed."

"He winked at me. You have any idea what it feels like to be winked at like that!"

"If you'd rather have the ticket—"

"That's not the point." She closed the bathroom door behind her, and stepped into the shower to wash away the humiliation. How could she possibly be that afraid of a little bird, and what twisted evolutionary impulse had her fucking on the side of the road? She was pissed.

"You were not exactly an innocent bystander!" he shouted at the closed door.

No matter how much water washed over her, she could not rid herself of the kestrel. She felt like it had in fact consumed some essential piece of her and she was trapped. Permanent prey to a bird who had long ago forgotten all about her.

She's with Eros. She can handle this. A little orgasmic comfort would fix it.

Instead of fighting the shower, she melted into it. She soaped her body and was reassured by how silky smooth she felt, not dead at all. Not even scared.

She began to relax, and touch herself. Almost absently at first, as if there was no urgency. As if she were not suffocating herself. As if she had surrendered too easily to the threat of dying, or had not battled it hard enough.

Well, she was back, she assured herself as the shower washed over any opposition. Death can go kiss its ass, she thought, she's taking a stand right here in the shower.

Her nipples responded instantly to her own caress. Her belly tightened as if showing off. Her clit resisted as if she were a stranger and the more determined her insistence, the more alone she felt.

When she couldn't make herself come, she was devastated. She felt like she'd been cut from the herd by a bird no bigger than a pigeon. Culled by the eyes of a hunter.

She gave up. When she finally emerged, she was fully showered and fairly stoic. He was lying on the bed and she joined him. "It's true," she volunteered, "I wasn't just a bystander."

"No."

She kissed him, by way of honoring her complicity. "I really had you going, didn't I?"

"Going?"

"Hot."

"Ah," he connected, recognizing that moods and attitudes seem to have shifted once again, though you can never be sure.

He kisses her.

She sighs. She tries for even the slightest moan but just can't come up with it. "I don't know, I'm just...I don't know."

"Yes you do. Just relax, it'll come back to you."

"I keep seeing that asshole winking at me," she explains because she still can't own up to the kestrel and all that it inspired.

"First of all," he says, willing to say anything to make her happy, "I think he was gay and he was winking at me. And if you must know, I was flattered."

That fucking does it. She cracks up. "Okay," she is finally able to say. She can't tell him that of all the times he has made her come, this is the one that counts. Because if the hawk had taken this from her, the rest too would fall away. Life once more crushed by death. Eros laid to rest by Thanatos. All because of that fucking bird.

"Roll over, I'll do your back," he offers.

"God, who would have thought horny could be such a fleeting thing."

He lifts her towels away and after warming his hands with fresh-brushed breath, he lays them gently on her back. Even with a light touch he can feel the knots retreat and resist.

Slowly. In long sensuous strokes that almost have her thinking not at all, other than the background drumbeat of *fuck you bird. Fuck you. Fuck you.*

"I've never felt your back so tight."

"Me too."

"Yup," he says, still kneeling in a slightly awkward position.

"Are you okay like that?

"I'm perfect. A few more minutes and I'll have you crawling all over me again."

God she hopes that's true.

He kisses and nibbles his way down to her belly from her firmly attentive nipples, and the phone rings.

"Shit," he hisses, the sound of an idea losing steam.

"The thing'll get it," she calms, and it does. Third ring.

"I give up!" he announces, as if the mood and the spirit had simply evaporated.

But she was not about to allow his pride to ruin the day. "Tell me a story."

"What?"

"Fly me away."

She moves in close and wraps her arms around him. She thrills to the warmth of his skin and the strength of his body pressed close.

She clamps her legs around his thigh, pulled close to her. She whispers back to him that his leg has become her favorite sex toy.

She will now surrender the fucking bird and is in desperate need of passionate carnal connection to restore her, to restore the wild animal that must still be in her, the part the kestrel didn't get.

"Okay close your eyes."

"They're closed." She was feeling just a tiny bit impatient, a tiny bit shy even after all these years. With a sigh she let go of the tension in her shoulders and her arms.

"My eyes are closed," she whispers seductively, trying to get this thing on track.

Lying on their sides, he enters her.

She cries out softly, an almost private sound, as a lullaby and it fills the room with pleasure.

It happens so quickly, almost accidentally, it surprises them both.

She opens her eyes. "Jack," she confesses, "I don't think—"

"Close your eyes."

"They're closed," she says, closing them.

"You're floating," he whispers.

"I'm what?"

"You're floating." He repeats. "Just imagine."

"Oh. Right. "

"The water is warm. The sun is hot," he tells her as he fucks her slowly.

"Yes."

"Yes?"

"Yes."

"You're weightless, dreaming. You think you're alone until someone glides by underneath you."

"What?"

"His slippery back barely touches yours."

Surprised, she moans, which in turn surprises her.

"You close your eyes."

"They are."

"No, in the water, you close your eyes so you can't see who it is."

"It's not you?"

"You're floating. Weightless. It feels like you're flying. Soaring, bathed in the close attention of the warm water that suspends you."

"Oh, Jack." She has no idea what he will say to her, what he'll do to her but she hungers for it. She trembles in anticipation.

"Oh."

"He runs his hand down your leg—"

"No. Who?"

"And back inside your thigh." He whispers softly so that she has to strain to hear, and the greater the strain, the deeper the immersion. The softer he speaks, the deeper she hears it.

Still inside her, barely moving, he can feel the pulsating roll of cunt ingesting cock, absorbing it. It is the mystery of the vaginal vespers that the greatest triumph is celebrated in surrender.

She holds tighter onto Jack. Pulls him deeper in. From a less intimate perspective, it might not look like the rambunctious calisthenics of movies or the cloying suggestiveness of television, but more like a couple of somewhat realistic mannequins pasted to-gether, belly to belly.

Up close, in the bed, skin to skin, heartbeat to heartbeat they are in perfect sync. He is paying per-fect attention, and she is humming pleasures because she trusts so completely that he will make her come so hard and so long that she will never think of an-other bird again.

"My eyes are closed," she reminds him because she desperately needed to get on with it, and she didn't want him to lose focus.

"He stands behind you," Jack was quick to re-spond.

"Uh-huh."

"He puts his arms around you, he rests his hands on your slippery, wet belly."

She moans. "Oh, Jack."

"He unties your top and lets it float away. He slips the bottom off and pulls you closer. You feel his hard cock against your back."

She shivers, and squeezes.

"Yes," Jack assures her.

"Oh God," she groans, no longer caring who it is that has her.

"A woman drifts up to you."

"A woman?"

"Slippery and glistening. She moves in close, her belly to your belly, her tits to yours."

Disturbed and somewhat astonished by how much this is turning her on, she opens her eyes. "Jack, I can't---"

"She's already kissing you."

"Jack, oh."

"You're safe. They're here for you. For having. For taking."

And with that she feels the gates primed to open. It startles her and she screams, and then she moans a sound so feral she doesn't even realize it comes from her.

"They kiss you, and stroke you."

"Yes."

"You stroke back, kiss back."

Her body shakes. A temblor. She has to breathe faster to keep up. There is no longer any distinction between the fantasy and the fucking.

"Yes?" Jack tests.

"Yes," she can barely say. Doesn't want to. Can't think of words anyway.

"She holds you from behind, floating you, her breast comforts your head."

"I've never been with a woman," she feels compelled to explain.

"Until tonight. She floats you and holds you in place for him. She has one hand on your tit, the other on your clit. He's going to fuck you silly, she tells you."

"I think I've come enough."

"He spreads your legs and penetrates with a force that shakes you and scares you."

"No," she says panting furiously. "No," as she strains, screaming.

"Yes," he says, and Katy explodes in writhing, orgasmic bursts. Taking him with her.

Later, when they can speak again, she opens her eyes, and is embarrassed and thrilled, and exhausted. "Oh my God," she says, "how did you do that?"

He kisses her and touches her face.

"I love you!" she confirms.

"I love you too."

"No, I really really love you."

"Slut," he responds.

She laughs and falls asleep in his arms, thinking only that the kestrel is a really pretty bird.

— ◊ —

BESS ANDERSON
FIRST FEMALE MESSIAH

Bess Anderson was about to become the first female Messiah. Like so many Redeemers before her – essentially all men, though there have been gender confusions – she never expected to be called upon in an official capacity. She simply went about her life trying to be a decent human being. Like many of the would-be messiahs over the years.

Anointed is one thing, but she never thought that she'd have to do anything. There were always messiahs-in-waiting aplenty. In every generation. Rarely are any of them called to duty. And she was pretty sure all the others were better qualified than she was. She took comfort in that.

Jesus of Nazareth of course. Most famous of them. Of the one hundred and six men with messianic aspirations in Jerusalem at the time, only Jesus was called to wear the crown, admitting to only a very few that he had all his life had this irrational fear of thorns. Of the hundred and six, nine other than Jesus were genuinely pre-messianic, awaiting the call.

There were charlatans too of course, but most were genuine and sincere. A voice in their heads had appointed them, and it's difficult to resist the Voice of God claiming you as his only begotten son. Or even second begotten. It's humbling.

Nobody wants the job. Jesus certainly didn't want it. He didn't want to be made all righteous and holy and executed.

Neither did Bess.

She dropped the kids off at school and hadn't gone more than a couple of blocks when He was back. "I need you, Elizabeth," He said.

"Bess," she insisted. She hated Elizabeth.

God apologized. "Bess."

"Thank you. You do remember that today is Thursday."

"I'm trying to talk to you about the end of the world and you think I'm worrying about whether or not you're going to get the car to the garage."

"Brakes are important."

"How can anything happen to you when I'm right here in the car with you?"

"You're just in my head."

"Fine, get the brakes tested. Look around you Bess, the world is in terrible shape."

"Shit. I forgot to pick up the skates."

"She still skates?"

"Now I have to circle all the way back to Munroe's which means I'm going to miss the dry cleaner. Shit! And it's your fault."

"The world needs saving."

"Send Jesus."

"I can't. Not again. He's still really upset."

"Why me? I'm not even Jewish."

"For starters it's hard to find anyone who really listens."

"I am no messiah."

"I will make you one."

"So I can end up like the others, wasting away on skid row? I see them drunk and drugged and wasted, still claiming to have spoken personally with God and I have no idea if they are really broken prophets or just drunk."

"It doesn't have to be like that."

"Are they there because they said yes to you, or because they said no."

"We've had this discussion."

"Because they stepped up, or because they ran away? You have a very bad habit of expecting too much."

"Fine, you're right, most of their lives have been ruined because they stood up and proclaimed what I asked of them. For generations, for centuries, millennia, I have sent saviors and redeemers and poets and prophets, and most of them die in agony and disgrace."

"And I want to sign up for this why?"

"No, you don't. That's the problem. "

She'd been sitting at the green light for long enough to get people honking angrily. She gave them the finger and moved on.

"You were saying," she said out loud.

She was right of course. There have been a slew of heavenly inspired Messiahs, but not one yet has redeemed the world. Simon bar Kochba led a revolution and was also done in by the Romans. A few hundred years later, Moses of Crete convinced his Jews to follow him into the sea, like the original Moses, and return to Israel like their ancestors did. But the sea didn't part for them and they disappeared, until their bodies washed up on the shore.

"I was saying I need you."

"And I was saying no. You have a very bad history with your messiahs."

Simon Magus the levitating Samaritan believed he was the Christ, and that never ends well. Ann Lee, the Shaker princess, claimed to be the female Christ and pointed to herself as the embodiment of all the perfections of God and might have become the first official female Messiah.

"So?" Bess had a right to know.

"She got a little ahead of herself. A more contemporary Narcissus. I knew early on she couldn't handle it."

But there was no shortage of ammunition. Hong Xiuquan, who billed himself as Jesus' younger brother, ended up killing himself. Or Mirza Ahmad who claimed to be both Mahdi and Messiah. And the Latter Day Saints Arthur Davies, proclaimed as the reincarnation of Jesus Christ. Or Sabbatai Zvi, the apostate who proclaimed himself the Messiah, then converted to Islam.

"All you send," she tried to explain to God, "are false messiahs."

"No, no, no." That pissed Him off. "Failed, not false."

"At the messiah level," she insisted, "there's not much of a difference."

"You want me to stop trying?"

"No, just find someone else. I can't do what You want me to do. I can't be what You want me to be."

"You don't know what I want."

"You want me to redeem the world."

"Okay, so, whaddya say?"

"No." She parked and ran into the supermarket where He continued to press her in the aisles. "I'll protect you."

"Like You protected the others?"

"Don't press your luck, Elizabeth."

"Got it."

"I'll be with you."

"Hang on, I have coupons," she explained to the cashier.

"No hurry. How's your day?"

"I hope you're just asking to be polite."

"Absolutely."

"Then fine, of course, and you?"

"Just another fucking day in Paradise."

"Always nice to see you," Bess said as she gathered her bags.

"Say hi to Bobbi, I'll see her at the rink."

"She seemed nice," God said back in the car.

"Maybe she wants to be the Messiah."

"It doesn't work like that. It has to be you."

"There are billions of other people—"

"I'm trying to have this same conversation with all of them."

"Listen to me. I have three kids. Plus a very fine husband. I have only one day a week in which I am not driving one or more kids to one or more places. I teach two nights a week. I do all the shopping and most of the cooking. I volunteer. I visit my sister in jail every week. I would like to help, but I just don't have the time."

"I'm talking about saving the world."

"It's not a part-time job."

"You won't be alone."

"Please. You won't even carry the groceries."

"You can't bargain with God."

"You're a voice in my head."

"You didn't say just."

"I didn't mean just. I meant, I'm doing all I can to make the world a better place, to make it suitable for a Messiah."

"I don't see you preaching. Or shouting from the hilltops. I don't even see you tweeting, so just what is it you're doing?"

"I take care of my family. I teach them to be strong and merciful and loving. I try to be kind and generous to everyone I meet. And other than that, you saw my schedule."

"Okay, fine."

"I can learn to play piano or something if you're really into hymns and stuff."

"I already said fine."

"Just like that, fine?"

"If I can get everyone else to commit to that, you wouldn't need a Redeemer."

"We'd all be the Messiah."

"Nice," God said.

"Guilt-tripping? That's how you do it?"

"It's effective."

"Just what is it you want me to do?"

"Do justly, love mercy—"

"Hey! I can read. It's in the Bible, which by the way, as an instruction manual, stinks."

"Critics I have enough of. A little sensitivity to the author might be in order here."

"Self-publishing can be hard."

God laughed. "I get it," He said, which is a lot for someone who often doesn't get it.

Bess was flattered. She was never much for telling jokes, but if you can make God laugh, you're never going to experience anything quite so holy again. Even if it's all in your head.

People have made gods laugh from the beginning, but hardly on purpose, and those who did make the comic effort rarely got Him to even crack a smile. He never laughed for Moses. Or Jesus. None of the prophets seemed to have had a jolly time. Siddhartha almost, a couple of times in the days before he became the Buddha.

She sat in her car in the driveway overwhelmed. Giddy. Humbled. Heard. "I'll need a list," she explained.

"What kind of list."

"Of what exactly it is you expect me to do."

"You know, save the world."

It felt really nice to have her status as a worthwhile human being so definitively certified. "That it?"

"Well," her Voice told her, "actually the world's going to be okay, it's you people guys I'm concerned about."

"Then do something about it," she said.

"This time it's not my flood, it's yours."

Damn. It had been such a nice day, and now it all just made her cry, just a few tears trying to carry away the overwhelming sadness she felt. There was no angry God threatening us, this was our flood.

There was no way in heaven or hell to pray our way out of it. You break it, you own it. Her voice was right, she had to do something.

Her daughter came out to see what was holding things up and waved.

"Got to go feed the hungry," she found herself pleased to say. "Let's talk tomorrow."

— ◊ —

THE LETTERS

My mother died today. I held her hand. Some days earlier she'd entrusted me with seven envelopes, one for each of her children, all of us now grown, some with kids of our own. Her instructions were simple and direct. Before we did anything else – notify people, make funeral arrangements, prepare for the shiva – I was to hand out these individually addressed envelopes to my siblings.

For two weeks I was the custodian of something sacred but I had no idea what it was. Were these our final grades – *I'm disappointed in you, not as disappointed as I am in your sister, but really, you could have done better.* Or other terrible secrets.

I could have been a better son. I know that. But let me at least open my letter and explain. The temptation to somehow peek was relentlessly intense, but doing so would feel like reaching into the grave before she'd even died. So I waited. The others knew nothing of the notes, so I waited alone.

Until she herself announced to everyone that she'd entrusted them to me.

"Why him!"

With five sisters anything could at any moment become an essential feminist issue. Mom nipped it in the bud. "I picked him because he is the best organized and most responsible of you all."

It took a moment, but they all got it and chuckled with her. I however was not amused.

"You know your brother," she went on, and I could tell that I was about to be even less amused. "If I had given the letters to one of you, he would have taken it badly. Broken his heart."

"No. I'd be fine."

"You'd be crushed," she insisted.

An hour after she died I handed out the letters. All available siblings, freshly orphaned and stunned, gathered together to seek and share comfort. Penny was three thousand miles away saving her sons from their father so she could only be there by phone.

The notes were in random order and Macci got hers first. She opened it and scanned the contents. As she read, the enormity of the note began to sink in, and she knew at once what crap her mother was pulling here.

Psyche got the next note and was immediately alarmed. The blood drained from her face.

"Psyche, you okay?"

She was not. She pressed the note tight to her chest, afraid the rest of us might see it. It was a gesture clearly meant to save us, or at the very least spare us. She knew instinctively that the information would really screw up the family, probably destroy it.

I was at home in California when the text came through. *Come quick, Mother's dying.*

Come quick is the easy part. Soon as you try to translate that into the real world, it all comes a cropper.

"What does that mean?" Li wanted to know.

"Comes a cropper? I have no idea."

We put our lives on hold, and made hasty preparations to be with Mom.

Of course the minute you do something concrete you're faced with the hard reality that both God and the Devil are in the details. You phone for airline tickets: "I want the next flight out."

"And when sir, will you be returning?"

When would I be returning!? What the hell kind of question is that! What he was asking amounted to: On just which day will your mother die? And will you be staying over for the funeral as well?

So we drove. We packed our electronics, and clothes and other essentials and hit the road and didn't stop until we got there. Mom was sitting in the dining room, in the large old arm chair at the head of the table. She was obviously weak, but her color was good and her eyes still sparkled and she was in good spirits. She laughed when we arrived. And cried and laughed. She was surprised and delighted and she laughed and cried some more and could barely stop touching us.

She looked well, that was the tricky thing. The call that brought us here was fraught with "Come quickly", which conjures up images somewhat at odds with a woman full of laughter. Come quickly is bloodshot hollow eyes. Come quickly is loose sallow skin and haunting cries of pain. It is not laughter.

"You didn't have to come, you know. I'm okay," she says, satisfied now that she has gathered all her family around her. It gave her strength and peace. Our presence here was her assurance that her most important request would be honored: that there would be enough of us to take care of her at home and she wouldn't die in a hospital.

Mom had reeled in her offspring. We came to say goodbye, and to help shepherd her though it. We came bearing gifts of love and support, and she taught us daily about grace on the line between life and death.

I had seen people die before. I've seen them die slowly, and I've seen them die suddenly. I've seen them young and old, sick and healthy. I've seen them die by accident, or by design, in agony and in peace, but the death of my mother was the first time I had ever seen anyone blossom into it.

She changed our notions of dying and death.

"The secret of her dying," Li knew, "comes from how she lived."

With all the siblings, and their kids, now home, chaos reigned. Everybody talked, nobody listened. It sounded like the happy garbles of too many chicka-dees in a tree.

The first few days after we arrived were fairly easy for us. Everybody was friendly and helpful. With so many of us there it was fairly easy to draw up a duty roster that assured that at least one of us would be with Mom at all times, twenty-four hours a day. It was a triumph of lists over chaos.

Scheduling is a nasty business and it got bitter.

"Fine," Psyche announced. "So I'll lose a day's work and if that's the way it has to be then that's how it'll be. Let's just cut the crap and whatever it is it is, okay? Jesus!"

"That is not what I said," Frannie said, "I said on Thursday night I have to go to Samantha's school play, so why couldn't you do an overnight."

"For a change, you said. Why couldn't I do an overnight *for a change*, like everybody else is pulling hard time and I'm getting away with something."

"Go, Psyche," Lewis encouraged.

"No," she corrected him, "I'm saying I'm not getting away with something."

"Oh," Lew said grinning as he walked by and kissed her on the head. "Too bad."

Mom tried to make peace but no one was listening. "I don't need anyone to stay overnight," she said. Twice.

The second time, everything stopped. Silence descended. All eyes turned to her.

"Shut the fuck up," Psyche told her, "this has nothing to do with you."

Mom burst out laughing. Psyche could always make her laugh. As First Daughter, Psyche had special privileges. Even I – firstborn, first son, Prince pending – couldn't get away with the stuff she got away with. From the beginning.

"That's no way to talk to your mother," Carolyn objected.

"Of course not, it was your mother I was talking to. My mother is nice."

Mom laughed.

Carolyn was pissed, and turned on her. "Psyche's right, mix out. Someone is spending the night."

"It's not worth all this fighting," Mom insisted.

Carolyn was astonished. "Who's fighting?"

"Ma," Psyche said, "it's not—"

"Don't do that. I hate being called Maaaaa."

"Okay, <u>Ma</u>."

"Penny, smack her for me. Penny? Where's Penny?"

"I was just kidding, Ma".

"Me too," Mom answered, "but smack her anyway. Lewis?"

"We're trying to have a serious discussion," Carolyn announced. "It's not about who wants to spend the night, we all want to stay with you, it's the principle of the thing."

"That's right," Psyche quickly agreed. "The principle is that whatever I think is a good idea, she doesn't. Whatever I want, she wants me not to have."

"I'm honored to have raised such principled kids."

"You're missing the point," Psyche told her.

"I'm missing the point?" Mom shot back, "you have a ring in your nose."

It was Psyche's turn to crack up.

"You know," Frannie tried the word-in-edgewise thing, "if we all focused some positive energy into this instead of quibbling over—"

"Hey! Back off," Psyche dismissed her.

"Very nice," Macci jumped in because as twins they always had each other's back. "She has as much right to speak as you do!"

"Why?"

"What?"

"Why."

It was enough for Mom. "I want to go back to my bedroom."

"My schedule is completely flexible," I volunteered, "just slot us in wherever you need someone."

"Thank you very goddam much," Frannie fumed. "Was that necessary!? If you think it's so easy to make the schedule, here you do it.

"No, you're doing great. All I meant was—"

"I know what you meant! Men always mean the same thing: Here let me fix it, your feeble female brain can't handle it. Well I have news for you, I'm a woman and I'm doing a great job making the schedules."

"That's what he said," Lew dared to speak again.

"He did," Macci confirmed. "I heard him. You heard him too."

"No I didn't. Don't tell me what I heard or didn't hear."

"Can I go back to my room?" Mom asked again, and was once more rebuffed by the sound barrier.

Macci turned to Carolyn for support. "Did you hear him?"

"This has nothing to do with me, it's between them."

"Can we just get this finished? You said your schedule was flexible and I could slot you in for any shifts I needed to."

"Exactly."

"Well fuck you, I don't need this. I'm making the schedule and I'm going to slot you in wherever I want to.

"Fine. Do it your way."

"Could someone please help me to my bedroom?

"I do not need the condescension," Frannie made clear by handing her clipboard to Carolyn and stomping off.

Carolyn turned to me, bristling with accusation. "Was that necessary?"

Macci chased out after Frannie.

"The hell with her, Macci, " Psyche advised, "let her go."

She came back and in spite of all the help Frannie got from the rest of us, she managed to put together a schedule that worked for everyone.

The truth is, beyond all the raging sibling rivalries and all the venting (most especially apparent during the weekly scheduling meetings) Mom was getting extraordinary care and love. When it came to actually embracing her emotionally and spiritually as well as physically, we were mostly incredible.

I really didn't care which shifts I got slotted into. The only thing I really cared about was not drawing the last shift. The final shift. I did not want to be there when she died.

I would do whatever else was required of me without complaint. Of course since no one knew when exactly she was going to die, each week's postings inspired a jolt of terror. Usually, the more daytime shifts I drew, the better I felt. I thought she was a night person, that she'd never die in the daytime. Maybe others did too.

My first shift alone with her was terrifying. Every time she coughed or cleared her throat or moved a little funny, my heart leapt to my throat. It was as if every minor discontinuity heralded her death. She coughed! Ohmygod she's gonna die. She twitched. Ohmygod, this is it! She grimaced from a gas pain and I almost passed out.

Mom sat up. "I can't take this anymore."

"Ohmygod. What!"

"Every time I take a breath, you jump. You're scaring the hell out of me. If you can't relax, go home and let me have some peace and quiet."

"I didn't drive across a continent to give you peace and quiet."

"Okay then."

"That's not what I meant. I meant I'm not leaving you alone."

She patted the edge of the bed for me to come and sit beside her. I did and she took my hand and stroked it with a mother's familiarity and patience. "So, what is it?" she asked. "You're scared?

"Hell yes. Aren't you?"

"A little less every day."

"It's pretty much the opposite for me."

"It's wonderful that you're here."

Death for me, when I thought about it at all, was this terrifying lightless monster of horrible menace. Something that could just come along and snatch you away without so much as a knock at the door.

She seemed relaxed. "I want you to—" she suddenly screamed out in pain.

I screamed in response.

I got her the yellow pills and in a short time the pain began to subside.

"Better," she said softly, a little before it was really better. "And you look awful. If it's of any help to you, I'm not going to die tonight. I promise."

"So now you're a doctor?"

She wanted to laugh, but could only manage a smile.

She was true to her word. Since the time I was nine years old and witnessed the very sudden demise of our neighbor, death had been a labyrinth of endless dark and morbid tunnels. Over the next several weeks, Mom lit the passageways and pushed the monster back. She showed us that death was not all that powerful, that it was full of weaknesses and flaws. And she showed us a calm in the face of it that became positively radiant.

"When it's time," she told us with total confidence, "your father will come for me."

"And you'll tell me?"

"You'll know."

We rented an apartment for our stay here. It was a penthouse in a high-rise on the hill and had virtually a three-hundred and sixty degree view. We could see winter storms coming down the river, planes taking off and landing at the airport, the many lights and splendors of downtown, the full canopy of stars on some nights.

Long days turned to long tortuous weeks, all of which took place in the blink of an eye.

As her body grew more tired and less able to sustain her, her soul grew larger and brighter and shone like a beacon to anyone who came near. Friends and relatives, strangers, doctors and nurses all fell under her spell.

Even in a world bounded by cynicism and despair, in a time deconstructed by petty visions and incidental irritations, it is still possible for people to be worthy of the love they inspire.

Weeks later, at her funeral, dozens of the people who embraced me and offered their condolences also whispered that she was their closest friend. People who were in fact close to her, and people who hardly saw her but every couple of years or so, all whispered the same. She was my closest friend.

On the morning that she died, I was alone with her. The very circumstance I had tried so diligently to avoid, had me now securely entrapped. It was my nightmare unfolding in real time. I knew she was leaving because she was talking to my father, dead now several years.

While Mom believed that she would not die in a hospital, my Father believed the opposite: that he could not die in a hospital.

On the medical front he could best be described as a Born Again Patient. He believed. Truly. I have no idea what evidence he collected to sustain this belief, but he believed. Modern medicine was a science. This was the modern world, gone were the dark ages of hocus pocus, bahnkis and garlic and other ancient superstitions. Now we have technology on our side and solutions are just a need away.

"You're not going to say hello to your father?" Mom said.

"My father?" It was chilling. To the bone. She had said that's how I'd know she was leaving. That he would come for her.

"He's sitting up on the dresser. What's the matter with you!"

Oh God, I thought. I said. "Hi, Dad."

The thing is, he is the love of her life. He is the purpose. She loved her children with all of her heart and her soul, but her connection to him was something even more special. They just made us, lots of us, but they *found* each other. In a gigantic sprawling universe, they found each other.

She never forgave him for dying. This woman who forgave everyone and held no other grudges, could not forgive him for leaving her and death was no excuse.

"What? I didn't hear that," she said.

"You were sleeping." I told her.

"I was?"

"For a little while."

"Did you two have a nice chat?"

I had little choice. "He's worried about you," I said.

"Oh, my love, I'm fine. Don't worry. I'm feeling much better. Those pills are very good, but it's very lonesome without you in the house."

I don't know what she heard him say, but she smiled. "I know," she said.

I wished I could see him. I owed him so much that I never thanked him for. In all my years of growing up he never missed a hockey game I played in, or a high school football game or a play.

He was a great man and I wish I'd known enough in time to thank him. For so much. Examples? How about the day he built my bridge to manhood.

It was high school. I was in trouble. Most of the time. On this occasion, I had, along with my four guys, committed some horrible earth-shattering transgression that I was promised would live on my permanent record forever and ever. (Now of course, in this century, there is a permanent record and it will follow you all your life and way beyond. God cut it off at seven generations, but now in the digital cloud, seven generations is nothing. It is to be sneezed at.)

We were ordered to bring our fathers to school next morning. When I explained all this Dad, the father who was always there for me said no. "You got yourself into this," he explained, "and you're going to have to get yourself out of it."

Next morning everyone showed up with their fathers, except me. I was subject to a tirade of disapproval, of scorn for Dad's parenting, and the professional glare from the Vice Principal indicating that he intended to make me pay for this insolence for the rest of my life.

When they finally finished demonstrating their coq walks, I was asked if I had anything at all to say.

"My Dad said that if I was involved in what happened to poor Mr. Darcy, I should be a man and take responsibility." When I said those words, I couldn't have been more proud of myself or my father. I felt empowered. I was my own man now.

Got my ass kicked for it. "I'll show you responsibility!" the VP threatened, and just to be clear, it was not a hollow threat. My friends got light sentences, their fathers were shown great deference and appreciation. All the guys were sent back to class and I was suspended for a week like I was the only one responsible for greasing up Mr. Darcy's favorite chair and nobody ever thought that he'd sprain his back sliding off the chair.

So I got my stuff from my locker and was escorted out by the janitor. It was a lonely walk. Suspended man walking. Not so sure empowerment was all it was cut out to be. It felt more like shame.

I left the building with my heart proud and my head hung low. I heard him before I saw him.

"Wanna grab some pancakes before I have to get to work?" Dad asked.

He'd been waiting. I was never alone.

"Very proud of you," he said and put his arm around me and walked me away from the school so no one checking us from the windows could see me cry. "Wish I could have been that strong when I was your age."

I knew right away it wasn't true. He was always a giant. This was just the grown-up version of the boy my mother fell so wildly in love with that the first time he kissed her she thought she was pregnant.

So for all the opportunities I had previously missed, I turned to the very tall dresser upon which Mom said he was sitting and said, "Dad, thank you."

"I told you," Mom said to him, very pleased, "I told you he just wasn't good at saying it."

She squeezed my hand. It was the last time.

"He's waiting for me," she said to me.

She really meant she was waiting for me to let her go.

I could barely get the words out, but I did. "Yes," I said, "he's waiting for you." She brought me into the world, and I would usher her out. I told her stories. They made her smile.

"Yes," she said.

"Is my father here too?" she asked.

"They're all waiting," I assured her.

"Yes," she said.

She turned to Dad, to her place in the universe and she smiled and died.

I continued to hold her hand for a while. I don't know how long it was before I called Li and she called my siblings and we gathered in the living room staring at Psyche who clutched her note from Mom to her chest and wouldn't let anyone see it.

149

Clearly protecting some secret so dark it could never be spoken.

On the phone, Penny kept saying what's going on, what's going on. Why isn't anyone saying anything. Hello? Hello!

The envelopes were randomly shuffled and next up was Carolyn. I gave her the note, and she opened it and the blood drained from her face. Like the others, she would not share it. It was impossible to know what she was protecting.

"You're not going to read yours out either?" Lew protested. It wasn't so much the contents he was concerned with, as hearing his mother speak. He got his envelope next and was no less horrified than the others.

Something was very much amiss and Psyche, who was never comfortable with mysteries other than the ones she sprouted, had it. The silence was just too much to bear.

She held up her envelope. "That bitch," she said. "I get it."

"Get what?"

She burst out laughing. "We all got the same note," she said. "Mine says: *You were always my favorite. Don't tell the others.*"

"No, I am," Lewis laughed waving his note.

"It's me."

"It's me!"

Depending upon your perspective, the spell was either broken or cast. Mom wasn't dead an hour and we were laughing. As one in our mourning.

"I don't know," Psyche said of me, "she always acted like he was her favorite, but I don't think she really liked him." She laughed and burst into tears.

She curled up beside me and wept. Freshly minted orphans.

In the end it was comforting to know that I was Mom's favorite, and so were the others. I have the documents to prove it.

— ◊ —

RACHEL, RACHEL, AVENGING ANGEL

Vengeance is never a pretty thing and Justice doesn't always work like you might expect. For starters, you never know who's going to live and who's going to die.

For most of her much abused life Rachel just tried to stay out of everyone's way. Do whatever it was they wanted of her. Just stay quiet and take it. Just stay quiet and be grateful. Just be quiet it's only a fucking abortion. Just be quiet, I'll pay you back I swear. Just be quiet. It became her default survival tool. Just be quiet.

But the night she held that girl in the alley inspired almost paralyzing concern. The girl grabbed her wholly by the heart and Rachel felt compassion welling up in her from way deep down in the past where she'd buried it. It confused her and scared her, this business of feeling something. For the longest time she'd shut it all down and survived by being invisible.

She's had a humiliating life. Runaway at twelve. Pimped out a year later. Used and abused. Trafficked and beaten. Abandoned. Again and again. You can't help but wonder what's a nice Jewish girl like her doing in a life like this.

The notion that she had any worth at all had been pounded out of her. She became what they made her, a reviled pet, sex trade equivalent of a junkyard hound. Just another hooker. Just another junkie. Just another survivor, the term loosely applied. She had long ago surrendered her personal dignity, and all that protected her now was humility and shame,

So when she saw the girl shaking on the ground, her first response – though not her natural instinct – was run away. Just keep walking. But the girl whimpered and Rachel stopped.

Sixteen years old. Dumped in an alley as disposable waste. Rachel tried getting her to a hospital but it was life that was killing her and there wasn't much Urgent Care could do about that.

Rachel borrowed a blanket from a homeless guy down the alley who was as detached as if he were eating popcorn in a foreign language movie theatre.

"Oh," the girl said when Rachel touched her. "Oh please no more."

"No more," Rachel promised her, and wrapped her in the blanket and held her. "No more," she promised as the girl trembled in her arms.

The asshole down the alley did in fact call 911 on his cell. He didn't mind helping, he just couldn't get involved on a personal level. It was only a gesture anyway, no ambulance was going to come racing to this part of town in the middle of the night.

Rachel never pressed the girl, but they did talk and she learned her name and where she was from and she learned all about a man so monstrous the girl died with his name on her lips.

"Jimmy Jim," she whispered, "sold me to some ranch guy from Montana. I never been out of Farley's Meadow and Jimmy Jim ships me off like a hog —"

It awakened seeds in Rachel that had lain long dormant. When she was a child she felt like a hero. Knew she was. Every time she tied a towel around her neck for a cape and flew down the hall, she knew that to the very core of her being she was the daughter of prophets and poets, warriors and kings.

But she doesn't feel it much anymore. From time to time she appeals to the merciful God she remembers and in silence she cries out *free me, take my breath.*

She needs desperately to scream but only finds the voice to whimper.

Rachel came from a very strict background, an enclave of orthodox Jews out in the suburbs. They didn't dress in Chasidic formal wear, or grow sideburns and beards, and they certainly didn't mingle. Otherwise they were pretty much indistinguishable from everybody else. Unless you scratched the surface, which was pretty much impossible to do.

They were intolerant of outsiders – intruders all – and discouraged would-be converts. They were deeply committed to and very protective of each other. For the first twelve years of her life Rachel knew little of anti-Semitism, other than the Holocaust of course. For several of her neighbors it wasn't an historical recall, they were directly connected by blood and experience. Their families, in their lifetime.

She loved all of it. The songs. The dances. The joy. The sense of incorruptible connection to a loving community, and inviolable personal security – an apparent change in policy since the *Shoah*. She understood that they were chosen by God, and that there were rules attached. For very good reasons, she was told.

At the age of twelve, in the months before her *bat mitzvah*, Rachel was raped by three boys from her study class. They had caught her taking a shortcut home and raped her in the fields.

The community was utterly appalled to learn that such an event had occurred right among their own. There was no official action, but a whisper in such a tight little world can be swifter than the law, and a glance can cut as deep as a sword.

Her parents took her to the *shul* where she delivered a fully self-shaming proclamation in which she promised "God and everyone" that she would never let anything like that happen again.

But even that homicidal swipe at her sense of worth was not enough to soften any hearts. Boys will be boys, and girls evil seductresses – born to it with their innocent eyes and invitational hair, and those brains that make them so tricky.

She said rape, they said sorry, and she was banished from their midst. Shamed out of their presence. Ex-communicated by snicker.

At the age of twelve, Rachel was excised from her world. Abandoned and despised, she found herself hungry, desperate, bewildered and terrified in the city. The perfect Jewish Princess had in no time at all been transformed into a pumpkin.

Young Rachel, inspired and full of promise, found herself in a world completely alien to her. No money. No credit cards. No friends that would take her calls. No parent secretly watching over and caring for her.

She was alone. Colder and hungrier as the hours rolled by. Day Three marked her first professional blow-job. It was delivered in exchange for shelter from the rain in the back seat of a car, and a sandwich.

There weren't many secrets in this last ditch neighborhood and Rachel was quickly discovered and pimped around. She was bought, sold and traded often until she was rescued by a young full-blooded Dakotan who came in to fuck her one day after work and fell in love instead. They ran off together and he took her back to his family in Minnesota.

His name is not important because Rachel vowed never to speak it again. But his mother, Tantoo, was more mother to her than her own. Tantoo loved Rachel from the beginning. She loved how eager she was to learn. She was most deeply touched by how easily Rachel took to the dances and it went straight to her heart. She was the daughter Tantoo never had.

After four years without bearing a child, or even coming close, the full-blooded Dakotan whose name won't be spoken showed up with a new wife and Rachel was dismissed.

Tantoo pleaded with her son. "Keep them both," she offered. "Don't send Rachel away." She shed many tears, but finally held no sway in the matter.

Broken and bewildered, Rachel was back on the street with nothing but her suitcase. In it though was her treasure, a gift that felt sacred the moment she got it: Tantoo's ceremonial robes.

It was a promise that the bond between the two of them would never be broken – that she would always be her mother – and Rachel wondered where Tantoo was now.

Despite all those horrible ghastly years of Rachel chipping away at herself, all the aches and pains and abortions and humiliations that she carried with her everywhere, she was transformed doing the simplest righteous courtesy for this stupid fucking girl who was no stupider than she herself had been.

On the streets, on the phones, stag parties and porn flicks, Pornhub and private parties, there was hardly a dark alley that she missed. But she never felt anything like this until she held the girl in her arms and felt the life ebb out of her.

Rachel wept. For the girl, and for herself. She wept because there was no way for her to make the world right. She had no voice. No power. No influence. No plans. But she could not let this girl's death go unanswered.

She lit candles and prayed. She tried to remember official dialogue from childhood, but came up only with the flimsiest of fragments. The only candle she had was from a birthday cake, so she lit that and blew it out.

Sorely afraid, unable to escape, she finally embraced her destiny: put a stop to Jimmy Jim and save the girls he had not yet turned to cash.

Her only weapon was a child's faith that she would find her way.

She armored herself with dreams of prophets, and by suiting up in Tantoo's ceremonial finest. Scared witless she set out to bring justice to Jimmy Jim, and peace to the girl.

Farley's Meadow was almost the size of a small county and Jimmy Jim owned most of it. It took Rachel a couple of weeks to get there and when she arrived, she was almost immediately captured.

There was no real jail so she was locked up in the now defunct blacksmith's shop, in a large cage that was built to hold a young grizzly. The blacksmith hoped to train and sell him to some carnival or circus. Unfortunately for both the blacksmith and the town, the bear had other plans and one day killed the blacksmith and ate his ass before returning to the wild, which was after all, only a few hundred feet away.

At the age of sixty-two, and a worn edition at that, Rachel was pissed that she had walked the eleven hundred miles just to come to this, even though she didn't walk it all. She managed to thumb a few rides, but not like the old days. When she was young she could get a couple hundred extra miles out of any trucker with just the hint of a pending hand job, or maybe better if they made decent time. These days it seemed like nobody wanted to fuck an old lady in tattered tribal garb.

When she looked at her reflection, even dusty from the road, she saw a shamanic warrior looking back. She saw Tantoo in her corner. She looked for the strength that she would need to carry out her quest. She wondered if Daniel could spare some time from the lion's den to help out, or maybe David and his armies.

Nice visions but she knew she was doing this alone and it was clear enough that people driving by didn't see the heroic spirit on a mission, they saw only what she appeared to be, a creaky old hag on a bender.

It was an anxious time in the remote village of Farley's Meadow. Ever since Rachel appeared it had become, not spooky exactly, but on edge. A place where everybody knows that everybody knows some terrible shared secret that's about to burst. That's why this meeting.

"No, you can't just shoot her," Jimmy Jim said, settling something that he thought he had already settled. "We're not savages."

It seemed an odd perspective seeing as it was Jimmy Jim she came for and it was his boys who locked her up in the bear cage. He spoke with the confidence and authority of a man who owned pretty much everything as far as the eye could see, including this hotel in which he was hosting what passed for a Town Council meeting.

He would of course pick up the tab, and while it was a generous gesture, it was not an act of generosity, but a statement of contentment that comes from knowing that it all belongs to you. The land. The cattle. The trees. The damn chairs they were sitting on.

"What the hell we gonna do about her then?" the barber demanded.

"She's got everybody freaked," Preacher jumped in. He was nothing close to a religious man but he was the guy who read some bible stuff at local funerals and sang a hymn or two at weddings. Outside of that he was an ugly drunk who nobody liked, except for Jimmy Jim.

"We hold her until they send someone—"

"It's been three days!" Arnie One-Eye complained. "The cops don't give a shit about us up here."

"Maybe," Jimmy Jim reprimanded, "if you hadn't said you think she's a witch, they might have taken the situation more seriously."

"I also said angel," Arnie defended. "I said there were people who thought that."

And there were. Lots of folks thought she might be. Lord knows they'd been praying for one long enough.

"Angel!?" Preacher intervened, "she's not even a goddam Christian."

Three days earlier, as the legend goes, Jimmy Jim and his boys caught Rachel sneaking around by his house. They knew she wasn't just any old woman because she just suddenly appeared out of nowhere. Sort of materialized in the dusky fog.

"Saw it with my own eyes," one of Jimmy Jim's boys testified. "One minute there's nothing, then boom...no, more like poof...and there she was."

"You couldn't see her...because of the fog."

Another of the ranch hands pitched in. "You knew right off she was a witch or something. Fought like a damn demon when we grabbed her."

"She said she come for Jimmy Jim," the first one added. "That's why we locked her up."

"She have business with you, Jimmy Jim?" someone said, laughing her off.

"Never saw her before in my life," he answered. Truthfully.

It would come as no surprise to anyone that there might be people eager to do harm to Jimmy Jim, but no one was so stupid as to let their curiosity pry into his private affairs.

About Rachel however, there was a great deal of speculation. Lots of opinions. Witch. Demon. Spirit. Crazy old lady. And yup, angel.

The churched locals thought that she was a blasphemy and they worried that Jimmy Jim might have in fact captured a genuine angel and if he had, the town would pay dearly for it.

Most of the local locals, the ones with the deepest roots, thought she might be the spirit of some long dead shaman. Maybe even a miracle worker.

"You're all acting like a bunch of damn fools," Sweet Sugar Sally announced, looking straight at Jimmy Jim. She was the only person from here to sunset with the balls to stand up to him.

The only fully tenanted room in the hotel belonged permanently to Sweet Sugar Sally who entertained gentlemen friends three days a week (Wednesday, Friday and Saturday.) She was, it was commonly agreed, very talented and highly skilled. And very particular. Demand for her professional services was so great there was a waiting list just to get onto the waiting list. Men drove ten hours just to spend two with Sally.

She was also, apart from Jimmy Jim himself, the area's leading entrepreneur. About half the shops that didn't belong to Jimmy Jim, belonged to her and she had fourteen thousand paid subscribers to her on-line quilting bee. "She's just one crazy old woman but she's got you all so scared you're wetting your pants."

"Nobody's wetting nobody's pants," Jimmy Jim said trying to be a calming influence. "What you don't seem to recollect is that when she appeared at my place, a young calf saw her, keeled over and died."

"This the calf whose Mama wouldn't suckle it?" Sally said, dismissing his claim.

"No, he's right," the older of the two Sullivan brothers interceded. "The night they found that woman, my mule took sick. Gone by morning. I'm telling you, she's some kind of fucking witch."

Nobody seemed to remember the Sullivans having an extra mule but that got lost in the ensuing scramble for inclusion, and everyone had a competing contribution.

Two of my chickens just keeled right over not two minutes after Martha heard the news.

My wife got the worst belly cramps she ever had in her life and it's not even her time.

Everybody's hiding at home. Nobody's been in my shop since word got out.

My well's gone bad.

My satellite TV went down and I don't think it's going back up until we do something about her.

Jimmy Jim popped another nitroglycerin. There were people in Farley's Meadow and beyond who derived real satisfaction from his medical issues. It was gratifying to see his cold fucking heart finally turning on itself.

"Has anybody even bothered to feed her?" Sally demanded, disgusted. "You water your horses for chrissake!"

"Nobody's going in there. It's a proven fact that a witch can kill you with a look. A single look!"

"No, that's true," the barber supported.

"Absolutely," Preacher piped in. "They can kill you with a look even if they can't see you. Bible says up to half a mile away."

"Dammit, Preacher, it does not," Sally stopped him. "Nobody here's getting married or buried, so shut your filthy fucking mouth, there's a lady present," she emphasized by huffing up her tits.

"If she can kill my mule," the younger Sullivan explained, "from five miles away, just imagine what she can do up close."

Sally left the meeting early and angry, knowing that if she didn't attend to Rachel, no one would.

Sally was a little apprehensive about what she was going to find in the cage. Angels and demons and witches and all weren't her cup of tea. She didn't believe in them and so she had no fear of them, but you never know.

Sally's first glimpse stunned her. Rachel could easily be mistaken for, or in fact was, a certifiable lunatic in very worn and tattered, but once fancy, ancestral garb. "If you're an angel or a spirit or a cherub or something," Sally said, approaching cautiously, "you are one ragged and dirty one in bad need of a bath."

Rachel was chained in her cage by a leg iron in the back corner of the old shop. Her eyes were very sad, but she had carefully pinned a wildflower in her hair. "You got a cigarette?"

Sally did not.

"Nobody smokes anymore," Rachel complained, "it's like they think something else won't come along and kill 'em instead."

"I can find you some."

"No thanks, I don't smoke. Come closer, I'm not gonna eat you."

"They say you're a liar."

Rachel laughed.

"They say no woman that old can walk that far."

"Yet here I am."

"They say you just materialized in the fog."

"That makes a whole lot more sense, doesn't it."

"I'm not the one that needs convincing," Sally told her.

"While we're waiting, you better get over here and show me your tits."

"What?"

"Your tits."

Sally blushed. Those tits have been gawked at, fondled, rented, sucked, caressed, and have been treated and mistreated, but never before had they made her blush.

"Isn't that why you're here, you're worried about your tits?"

There was no way for Rachel to know this and so it instantly cut through all of Sally's defenses and as if in a trance, she did what she was told. She walked up to the cage and unbuttoned her shirt.

Rachel put her arms through the bars and caressed Sally's tits gently before she examined them more closely. Touching. Pressing. Following the discomfort up under her pecs. With the tips of her fingers she located exactly where the pain was coming from.

"Okay," Rachel finally announced, "it's not what you think. It's not the cancer and it's not gonna kill you."

While Sally drank that in and began to sob with relief, Rachel emptied some herbs from pouches on her belt. Not much more than half a lima bean's worth. She spit into her hands and made a paste, just like Tantoo had taught her.

She breathed on the paste to warm it and reached out between the bars and applied it. She explained it was just a cyst and this would help and Sally almost immediately felt the anxiety dissipate, taking some of the pain with it.

Back at the hotel Sally had a busy night scheduled and for the first time in a very long while took her work as a celebration. No cancer. The old witch said no cancer and Sally worked the night with joyous abandon. Especially for a Wednesday.

As it turns out, men on the verge will tell you just about anything if you'll just get on with it. The conversations were for her a shocking introduction to a kind of frontier justice she'd never really seen before. A primal fear steeped in magical paranoia gripped the valley.

Farley's Meadow was losing it. Off the fucking deep end. Two of her clients openly discussed "getting rid" of Rachel, as if it were a perfectly natural thing to be talking about with a hard-on.

The word on the street – although technically there wasn't much of a street to Farley's Meadow – was that the authorities weren't ever coming to collect Rachel, and even if they do, they'll eventually let her go and she'll come back, so they couldn't just set her free, for fear of reprisal.

Spirit or madwoman, real or not, the shared wisdom was that Rachel had done nothing but bring misfortune and misery to Farley's Meadow. There was Mrs. Lander's stillborn baby, couple of months before anyone here had even heard of Rachel, but it seemed to make the point anyway. And the fishing's been bad. And Joanna's chickens started losing their feathers and stopped laying eggs, like last year but worse.

And of course, the reason everyone was so tense in the first place, was the funeral of Laurie Little. Sixteen years old. They sent the body back up all the way from Los Angeles. The funeral was terrible. Everyone cried. She was the fourth one in the last few years to come back in a shipping box. The only one that Rachel knew.

The funeral was a couple of weeks ago but the town was still hurting so Rachel's timing turned out to be of some significance. So much so that it was creeping into Sally's boudoir, and that was completely unacceptable.

It came to a head, so to speak, when one of Jimmy Jim's closest aides came in for a blow job and said straight out that Jimmy Jim had decided that the old lady needed justice and there was no point delaying matters.

"What the hell does that mean?" Sally demanded, releasing his balls.

"You know. Not the first time you heard Jim calling for justice."

"He's going to shoot her!"

"No Ma'am. They're going to hang her. All legal like."

"She's an old lady!"

"Wouldn't say Lady," he said, "and no offense Ma'am but you gonna suck on that thing or just keep dangling it?"

"When is this supposed to happen."

"I can't say."

She stopped dangling. "I asked you when."

"Nobody told me nothing," he told her, realizing he had already told her much too much.

"Do I need to be telling people you waited three months for a date and when you finally got here you couldn't get it up?"

"Couldn't get it up?! What the hell you think you're looking at."

"Oh," she said because she couldn't resist, "is that it?"

"Fuck you. I'll just tell 'em it wouldn't fit."

"And I'll say it's because I'm a virgin, and they'll laugh you so far out of town you'll be in walking distance of the city."

"Ma'am, Sally, please. Ain't none of this my fault."

"Hon, you know I love you, and you know how much I want to make you happy, but I just can't get in the mood if all I'm thinking about is that poor old lady locked up waiting for Jim to kill her."

"Not kill, Ma'am. Absolutely legal," he insisted, "for up here."

"Legal or not, dead's dead."

She got off her knees and slipped a sweater on.

"No wait. What are you doing? Ma'am? Ma'am?"

"You have to go now."

"Like this. You're going to leave me like this!?"

"No, I'm not leaving. You're leaving."

"Tonight," he cried out desperately, speaking directly from the base of his cock. "Jim said tonight."

She thanked him for that, the old-fashioned way, with a handshake. She gave him back his money and sent him off whining in protest.

Wondering what she might need she gathered up a few essentials, including a pearl-handled pistol she had been given in gratitude some time ago by a man she now barely remembered.

"Afraid they're going to lynch me?" Rachel greeted her.

"Of course not," Sally lied because she believed that no one would harm Rachel if she was there as a witness. With a gun. "No, I just thought you could use a few things."

"I wouldn't worry so much about me," Rachel told her gently. "I didn't come here to get hanged."

"Why did you come?"

"For that girl you just buried."

"You knew her?"

"No. Just met her the one time."

"One old hooker to another, just tell me straight why the hell I'm here trying to protect you?" Waiting for an answer Sally got the blanket from her bag and offered it to Rachel who said no thank you I'm good and you're going to need it more than me.

Sally took that to be an invitation and she wrapped herself in the blanket and sat leaning against the cage. It shocked her when Rachel slipped out of the leg iron and came to sit beside her.

"How did you do that!"

"With a magical Chippewa chant that makes iron turn into rubber—"

"Into rubber!? Incredible."

"Oy, Sally," Rachel sighed. She was a little disappointed and hoped she wasn't just talking to an idiot. "You can talk to iron all you want, it's still going to be iron."

"But I saw you—"

175

"It's built for a damn bear, not a skinny old lady. I can slip in and out any time I want."

"People say you came here for Jimmy Jim."

"To kill him, yes," Rachel agreed.

"He says he doesn't even know you."

"For a long time now, Jimmy Jim's been sending teenage girls from all over the county to California, and other places, some so far away that coming home will never be an option. They were advertised as au pairs and housekeepers but they were slaves. The working dead."

"No." It was devastating.

"He helps them right into the trade. Even lends them a few bucks to get settled and uses them as toys until he's ready to sell them."

"I swear to you," Sally swore, "I never knew anything about any of this."

"Nothing?"

"Very little."

"Everyone knows *dead man walking*. Movies. TV. Newspapers. But nobody talks about *dead girls fucking*. Kids whose lives are all but over, used up in a hell hole and left in the gutter to die."

"Oh, God," Sally whispered.

"I'm here to put a stop to him."

Still reeling, Sally was overwhelmed. "What the hell do you think you can do to Jimmy! Nothing. You're a washed out old street whore locked up in a cage. There's no way you'll even get close to him."

"He'll come to me."

"I have a gun," Sally offered.

"I don't need your gun."

"If there's anything Jimmy cares about, it's his reputation, and he isn't going to let—"

"I wasn't going to ask permission."

"He's obsessed with his legacy, with becoming—"

"He's going die in shame," Rachel promised.

"I can stop this without bloodshed. People will listen to me."

"You think they love you because you fucked half of them! They love you because you give them something to look down on."

"Ain't that the truth," Sally quickly agreed. "The People are always kind to me, it's the settlers, the poachers, pale-faced trash like me that's always making me feel like dirt. What the hell did I ever do to them?"

"And Jimmy Jim?"

"He comes by once a month to collect the rent."

"Ah."

"He's usually pretty quick about it. Efficient. Look, the only reason you're still alive is because I'm here and they're afraid to come in and have to deal with me. Not a one of them wants their secrets made public."

"That's very sweet of you. I don't get a lot of that. When I was young and beautiful, and I was, everyone was sweet to me. Not only men trying to get into me, but everybody."

"If I can get you through the night...there's a bus in the morning, only comes twice a week, and I just want to make sure I get you on it alive."

"You're a good whore, Sally, and I appreciate your company, but really, it's not me you need to be worrying about. It's them. They're all riled up and they're coming this way."

Sally checked her pistol. Hadn't fired it in years, not since she shot old Ralphie Digug in the knee. She felt terrible. She'd been aiming for his heart and after that she didn't much trust guns and she was pretty sure lack of practice hadn't made her a better shot.

The mob announced itself with unintelligible shouting and the even more disturbing sound of guns fired into the air. Sally was scared and flinched each time she heard the men trying to ram the big doors she had wisely bolted.

The fury eventually rose to clearer snippets, flecks of rage exploding from the noise. *Give us the witch. Open the doors. Burn her out! Pour water on her!*

"Pour water on her?" Rachel puzzled.

"Wizard of Oz," Sally reminded her, "they melt the bad witch."

Rachel chuckled. "Oh no, don't get me wet. Oh help oh help." Rachel was enjoying herself and Sally couldn't help but surrender to the angelic ease that came with Rachel's smile.

The attack had begun with a handful of Jimmy Jim's guys deciding they were going to do Jimmy Jim a favor and put an end to this terrible discomfort everyone was feeling. Just end the damn problem.

As Jimmy Jim's men paraded down the road to the old blacksmith shop, the noise and enthusiasm attracted others and by the time they got to the place, they were a mob. Not perhaps by urban standards, but thirty, thirty-five people in Farley's Meadow certainly qualifies as a mob.

A couple of rounds of buckshot bounced off the big steel doors and then everything went quiet outside, replaced by the arrival of Jimmy's huge tractor.

Without much ado he went straight for the doors and took them clean off their hinges.

Sally stood fast with her gun which was enough to convince those who wanted to rush in, not to.

Finally, Jimmy Jim got down from his tractor and walked straight into the cavernous shop. "Put your damn gun away, Sally. Not going to do you any good."

He was right about that. Truth is, his advice to her had always been good, and she trusted him but that was before she knew. Now something in her belly warned her not to put the gun away.

"Slaves?" Sally charged. "You sold those girls as slaves!"

"Is that what the old witch is telling you?"

"Hookers. On the goddam street!"

"That's crazy," Jimmy Jim turned to announce to the mob following him in.

"Then how come my Robin don't call no more," a voice demanded.

"In-home baby-sitting and pussy service," Sally continued.

"The witch poisoned her, she's loco," someone said stepping forward in support of Jimmy Jim. Didn't even work for Jimmy, was just a local guy, Angus

Bouchard, who was terrified by the rumors and just wanted this whole sordid business done before it did any damage to his kids.

"Really, Angus, really? Nobody fed me any poison and she's not a witch. Are you really going to force me into talking publicly about...private things? With your lovely wife screaming like a maniac beside you?"

Mrs. Bouchard stopped shouting immediately.

"And wouldn't you like to step back with the others, Mr. Bouchard?"

Yes, he'd like that very much and hung his head and stepped back trying to avoid his wife's eyes.

"You can tell she's done something to Sally," Jimmy Jim announced with great authority. "Don't listen to her."

But people were listening. It was about their children. Their dreams. Their hearts.

Jimmy realized it was a bad idea to be here but the mob of support behind him was now an impenetrable wall, many families deep. He wasn't going anywhere.

Attack was the only answer. He strode up to the cage ready to accuse Rachel but he never got a chance. As he reached the cage and grabbed hold of a couple of bars, Rachel rose slowly from her shackled corner.

The room went silent. She walked toward Jimmy Jim who was doing everything he could not to shit his pants.

Stopped by the chained leg, she paused for effect. On impulse, she chanted out some mumbo jumbo before she slipped her foot. People gasped. A few screamed. Several left immediately at this incontrovertible display of otherworldliness.

Jimmy Jim, he backed away. He was scared. He was sweating. He was breathing hard and there was a ghostliness in his face.

Suddenly Rachel shrieked. It was all her silenced years of enforced whisper cutting free. She unleashed a sound so powerful and penetrating, it felt like the walls of hell had fallen away. It felt like salvation.

She could barely believe the sound was coming from her and she marveled at it. This was the sound of imposed silence breaking free.

It was a screech of such fearsome power and fury, so much bigger than she was, it could only be, she believed, that the prophets and poets, warriors and kings, had her back.

She grew louder and more piercing by the moment, and it went on and on as if she had no need of breath.

People ran. Some fainted. Others cried in pain.

Jimmy Jim fell to his knees in front of the cage, holding his ears, frozen in agony. He could feel his heart thump and thunder and finally managed to take the key from his vest pocket and throw it into the cage.

Rachel's shriek went silent as suddenly as it had begun, leaving some damage in its wake. Sally was in awe and Jimmy Jim was on his knees too scared to move. He was clammy and nauseous.

Rachel stepped from the cage, dancing.

Slowly. Like Tantoo had taught her.

Chanting as she danced, the only holy prayers were from her childhood and all she really remembered were bits and pieces.

You could feel the drums in her footsteps. You could see the prophets in her song. You could feel the holy rise in her.

She danced around Jimmy Jim, in a wide circle and he cried out, "Somebody. Help me."

No one dared to violate the circle Rachel prescribed.

"They're coming for you," she said in a whisper everyone could hear. Your fathers and their fathers.

"*Hipla bana konnotsh boma hoo*" she chanted as she danced around him.

With every syllable he could feel the grip on his heart squeeze tighter. He understood not a word of it because he spoke not a word of anything but English, but he knew what it meant. He knew he was going to die if she didn't stop.

Rachel also didn't understand a word. They were just sounds that came to her and seemed to speak to God. Sometimes a phrase or two she remembered from the Holidays – *boray pree hagoffen* – supplemented by rhythmic babble – *hoo gallaalal chickaba.*

It turns out the words didn't matter, it was the sound of her lifelong agonies wailing to the skies, and old Jimmy shit his pants. Actually.

His chest tightened like a cinch and breathing was hard. Very hard. And dizzy. He couldn't find the nitroglycerine he always carried in his pocket.

"I never meant to hurt anybody," he confessed, barely able to get the words out.

And Rachel danced and chanted. Round and round. His face grew red and twisted. Round and round.

He turned to see the families he had betrayed, to ask for their intercession, to beg for mercy but when he saw their faces he felt nothing but suffocating shame.

Rachel danced and chanted and even knowing all the babble was babble, she too was transformed by it. Transported by it. She was as trapped in this death dance as Jimmy Jim.

She thought of nothing but the dance. She knew that she had to keep dancing or her universe would cease, unravel from here to Adam and Eve.

Jimmy Jim cried out, oh God no.

And Rachel's dance ended abruptly. The final step came so suddenly that even she wasn't expecting it. Her foot hit the ground with a whomping thunder, and it was done.

She froze, and Jimmy Jim toppled dead to the floor.

You can't always tell if a miracle is a good thing or not, but the relief Rachel felt was incontestable. An entire lifetime gone wrong suddenly fled from her shoulders. The dance had restored her to herself. Her back stopped hurting, her eyes stopped blurring, and she finally remembered what it felt like to be a child, to feel free. To actually be happy.

She would have wept with joy, but couldn't with all those people staring at her, all too scared to get too close.

They made a wide berth as Rachel began her exit. Some dropped to their knees, bowing to the angel who had avenged their children.

Three of Jimmy Jim's guys slipped out and Sally panicked. She figured she knew exactly what they were up to. They'll find a dark stretch of road and ambush Rachel. Cut her down in the dark.

"Don't go out there," Sally called to her. "Don't go out there."

But Rachel went. The bleak and scary street was nothing new in Rachel's life, which meant she knew enough to be afraid.

With every step, she felt freer and lighter and more whole than she had since she was a child.

She was exhausted, but managed, one foot after the other. Don't look back. Don't look back. The highway became the torch of her redemption, the recognition of her sacrifice. All she had to do was make it there.

Rachel hadn't gone a hundred yards when she heard the pick-up coming down the road behind her. It cut her off and Jimmy's three guys jumped out.

"Oh no," she cried, frozen in the headlights. "Not now," she pleaded. "Not now."

"Right now, witch," the one with the club hissed.

The third one cracked his shotgun and loaded up.

Vengeance is not a pretty thing. And they were not going to let her die easy. The guy with the club stepped forward, aiming for her belly.

"Do I need to kill you too?" Rachel glared at him.

It stopped him. He didn't really believe she had any powers, he didn't believe in that crap. On the other hand Jimmy Jim was dead, so he lowered the club and stepped back.

"Jesus," Shotgun muttered, "you're afraid of an old lady?"

"She ain't just any old lady."

With that, Rachel let out a shriek. She did the only thing she could, she danced and she chanted. *Boray baruk over troubled waters hochelaga.*

It was a mistake. The avenging angel who came for Jimmy was as gone as he was. Out there on the road she was just an old lady with a sore back and tired legs. It was supposed to scare them, but they laughed.

"Screw this," Shotgun announced, "let's just finish it."

He was about to blow Rachel away when he heard the first of the Hallelujahs.

Hallelujah, they sang. Half the town. Recognition that not all angels come from the sky. *Hallelujah*.

They surrounded Rachel, and sang – *Hallelujah, Hallelujah*.

Rachel rid Farley's Meadow of a strain of generational evil, but there is no record of her. The reports of Jimmy Jim's death, an event of some significance in the valley, all spoke of cardiac arrest.

No mention is made of Rachel.

The night is rarely discussed in town but when it is they talk about the time an avenging angel came to the valley in rags and was persecuted for not looking like what they thought an angel should look like.

Now they try to treat everyone with dignity. Just in case.

— ◊ —

ACKNOWLEDGEMENTS

My enduring awe and gratitude to Alicia and Jessica, for their immeasurable contributions and relentless support.

And my deepest appreciation to my patient draft-in-progress readers who entrusted me with their deepest thoughts and responses – Elaine Dewar, Stephen Dewar, Charles Greene, Randi Johnson, Irving Meyer, Joanna Migdal, Ralph Phillips, Maxine Ruvinsky, Penny Ruvinsky, Danny Singer, Tisha Singer, and Tom Szollosi. Thank you all.

MORRIE RUVINSKY *is an award-winning writer and filmmaker with several movies and television series to his credit.*

He lives in California with his wife and partner Alicia, in walking distance of daughter Jessica and son-in-law Michael.

Dream Keeper
(a novel)

**Los Angeles Times
Best Books of the Year**

"Part myth, part thriller, part song. It is transporting."
–Susan Salter Reynolds

Meeting God or Something Like It
(short stories)

Whether God is pulling the strings or is just the Great Placebo in the sky, all these stories – the ones that make you laugh and the ones that make you cry – share a common perspective: It's never about God. It's always about us.

A Father's Son
(a novel – coming soon)